WANTING HIS
CHILD

WANTING HIS CHILD

BY

PENNY JORDAN

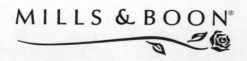

MILLS & BOON®

First published in Great Britain 1999
Large Print edition 1999
Harlequin Mills & Boon Limited,
Eton House, 18-24 Paradise Road,
Richmond, Surrey TW9 1SR

© Penny Jordan 1999

ISBN 0 263 16172 2

Set in Times Roman 16½ on 18½ pt
16-9909-48260 C1

Printed and bound in Great Britain
by Antony Rowe Ltd, Chippenham, Wiltshire

CHAPTER ONE

VERITY MAITLAND grimaced as she directed the long nose of the top-of-the-range BMW sports car she was driving through the outskirts of what had once been her home town.

It may have been over a decade since she had originally left but, from what she could see, nothing much seemed to have changed—but then why should it have done? Just because so much had changed in *her* life, that didn't mean…

The car was attracting a good deal of covert attention, and no wonder: from its immaculate shiny paintwork to its sporty wheels and its sleek soft-top hood it screamed look at me… admire me…*want* me.

She would never in a thousand years have deliberately chosen a car so blatantly attention seeking and expensive and had, in fact, only bought it as a favour to a friend. Her friend, a modern wunderkind spawned by the eighties, had recently taken the decision to 'downsize' and move herself, her man, and her two children to a remote area of the Scottish Highlands where, as she had explained ruefully to Verity, the BMW would be a luxury she simply couldn't afford. What she had also not been able to afford had been the time to look around for a private buyer prepared to pay a good price for the almost new vehicle and so, heroically, Verity had stepped in and offered to buy the car from her. After all, it was hardly as though she couldn't afford to—she could have afforded a round dozen or so new cars had she wished.

Along with the nearly new car she had also acquired from the same friend a nearly-new wardrobe of clothes, all purchased from Bond Street's finest.

'I'm hardly going to be wearing Gucci, Lauren, Prada or Donna Karan where we're going,' Charlotte had sighed, 'and we are the same size.'

Well aware, although her friend hadn't said so and despite her cheerful optimistic attitude, that her 'downsizing' had not been totally voluntary and that money was going to be tight for her, Verity had equally picked up on Charlotte's hints about selling off her wardrobe and had stepped in as purchaser.

She could, of course, have simply offered to give her friend the money; as a multimillionairess, even if only on a temporary basis, she could after all afford it, but she knew how Charlotte's pride would be hurt by such an offer and their friendship meant too much to her for her to risk damaging it.

'After all, it isn't just *me* who's being done a favour,' Charlotte had commented enthusiastically as they had stood together in the large bedroom of her soon to be ex-Knightsbridge house, viewing Verity's appearance in the white Gucci trouser suit she had just pulled on.

'Now that you've sold the business and you aren't going to be working non-stop virtually twenty-four hours a day, you're going to need a decent wardrobe. You're going to have to watch out for fortune hunters, though,' she warned Verity sternly. 'I know you're in your thirties now, but you're still a very attractive woman...'

'And the fact that I'm currently worth over forty million pounds makes me even more attractive,' Verity suggested dryly.

'Not to me, it doesn't,' Charlotte assured her with a warm hug. 'But there are men...'

'*Please*... You sound just like my uncle,' Verity told her.

Her uncle. Verity was thinking about him now as she drove through the town and headed out towards her destination. It had been an ironic touch of fate that the very house where she had grown up under the guardianship of her late uncle should have been one of the ones the estate agent had sent her details of as a possible house for her to rent.

When people had asked her what she intended to do, having finally taken the decision to sell off the business she had inherited from her uncle—a business which she had been groomed by him to manage and run virtually from the moment she had gone to live with him following her parents' death; a business which she had been brought up by him to look upon as a sacred trust, as the whole focus of her life and as something far, far more important than any personal desires or needs she might have—she had told them, with the calmness for which she was fabled, that so far she had made no plans. That she simply intended to take some time out in order to give proper consideration to what she wanted to do with the rest of her life. After all, at thirty-three she might not be old, but then neither was she young, and she was certainly wise enough to be able to keep her own counsel—it was not completely true that she hadn't made any plans. She had. It was just that she knew exactly how her advisers, both financial and emotional, would look upon them.

To divest herself of virtually all of the money she had received from the sale of the company was not a step they would consider well thought out or logical, but for once in her life she wanted to do what felt right for *her*, to be motivated by her *own* judgement rather than simply complying with the needs and demands of others.

She had fought a long battle to retain ownership of the business—not because she had particularly wanted to, but because she had known it was what her late uncle would have expected—but that battle was now over. As she herself had known and her financial advisers had warned her, there had been a very great danger that, if she had not accepted one of the excellent offers she had received for the sale of the business, she could have found herself in a position where a sale had been forced upon her. She had at least managed to ensure that her uncle's name remained linked to that of the business for perpetuity.

Verity frowned, automatically checking her speed as she realised she was approaching the local school and that it was that time in the afternoon when the children were coming out.

It was the same school she had attended herself, although her memories of being there were not entirely happy due, in the main, to

the fact that her uncle's strictness and obses-
sion with her school grades had meant that she
had not been allowed to mingle freely with her
classmates. During the long summer evenings
when they had gone out to play, she had had
to sit working at home under her uncle's eagle
eye. It had been his intention that her father,
who had worked alongside him in the business
and who had been his much younger brother,
would ultimately take over from him, but her
father's untimely death had put an end to that
and to the possibility that he might have further children—sons.

Her uncle's own inability to father children
had been something that Verity had only discovered after his death and had, she suspected,
been the reason why he had never married
himself.

She was clear of the school now and the
houses had become more widely spaced apart,
set in large private gardens.

Knowing that she would shortly be turning
off the main road, Verity automatically started
to brake and ten seconds later was all too

thankful that she had done so as, totally unexpectedly, out of a small newsagent's a young
girl suddenly appeared on a pair of roller
blades, skidded and shot out into the road right
in front of Verity's car.

Instinctively and immediately Verity reacted, braking sharply, turning the car to one
side, but sickeningly she still heard the appalling sound of a thud against the front wing
of the car as the girl collided with it.

Frantically Verity tugged at her seat belt
with trembling fingers, her heart thudding with
adrenalin-induced horror and fear as she ran to
the front of the car.

The girl was struggling to her feet, her face
as ashen as Verity knew her own to be.

'What happened? Are you hurt? Can you
walk…?'

As she gabbled the frantic questions, Verity
forced herself to take a deep breath.

The girl was on her feet now but leaning
over the side of the car. She looked all right,
but perhaps she had been hurt internally,

Verity worried anxiously as she went to put her arm around her to support her.

She felt heartbreakingly thin beneath the bulkiness of her clothes and Verity guessed that she wouldn't be much above ten. Her grey eyes were huge in her small, pointed white face, and as she raised her hand to push the weight of her long dark hair off her face Verity saw with a thrill of fear that there was blood on her hand.

'It's okay,' the girl told her hesitantly, 'it's just a scratch. I'm fine really... It was all my fault... I didn't look. Dad's always telling me...'

She stopped talking, her eyes suddenly brimming with tears, her whole body starting to shake with sobs.

'It's all right,' Verity assured her, instinctively taking her in her arms and holding her tight. 'You're in shock. Come and sit in the car...'

Glancing up towards the shop the girl had just come from, she asked her gently, 'Is your mother with you? Shall I...?'

'I don't have a mother,' the girl told her, allowing Verity to help her into the passenger seat of the car where she slumped back, her eyes closed, before adding, 'She's dead. She died when I was born. You don't have to feel sorry for me,' she added without opening her eyes. 'I don't mind because I never knew her and I've got Dad and he's...'

'*I* don't feel sorry for you,' Verity assured her, adding with an openness that she could only put down to the fact that she too was suffering the disorientating and disturbing effects of shock, 'I lost *both* my parents in a car accident when I was six.'

The girl opened her eyes and looked thoughtfully at her. Now that she was beginning to get over her ordeal she looked very alert and intelligent and, in some odd way that Verity couldn't quite put her finger on, slightly familiar.

'It's horrid having people feeling sorry for you, isn't it?' the girl said with evident emotion.

'People don't mean to be patronising,' Verity responded. 'But I do know what you mean...'

'Dad told me I wasn't to go outside the garden on my rollers.' She gave Verity an assessing look. 'He'll ground me for ages—probably for ever.' Verity waited, guessing what was coming next.

'I don't suppose... Well, he doesn't *have* to know, does he...? I could pay for the damage to your car from my pocket money and...'

What kind of man was he, this father, who so patently made his daughter feel unloved and afraid? A man like her uncle, perhaps? A man who, whilst providing a child with all the material benefits he or she could possibly want, did not provide the far more important emotional ones?

'No, he doesn't *have* to know,' Verity agreed, 'as long as the hospital gives you the all clear.'

'The *hospital*?' The girl's eyes widened apprehensively.

'Yes, the hospital,' Verity said firmly, closing her own door and re-starting the car.

She would be being extremely negligent in her duty as a responsible adult if she didn't do everything within her power to make sure the girl was as physically undamaged as she looked.

'You have to turn left here,' the girl began and then looked closely at Verity as she realised she had started to turn without her directions. 'Do you know the way?'

'Yes. I know it,' Verity agreed.

She ought to. She had gone there often enough with her uncle. Before he had moved the company's headquarters to London, the highly specialised medical equipment he had invented and designed had been tried out in their local hospital and Verity had often accompanied him on his visits there.

One of the things she intended to do with the money from the sale of the company was to finance a special ward at the hospital named after her uncle. The rest of it… The rest of it would be used in equally philanthropic ways.

That was why she had come back here to her old home town, to take time out to think about what she wanted to do with the rest of her life and to decide how other people could benefit the most from her late uncle's money.

When they arrived at the casualty department of the hospital they were lucky in that there was no one else waiting to be seen.

The nurse, who frowned whilst Verity explained what had happened, then turned to Verity's companion and asked her, 'Right... Let's start with your name.'

'It's... It's Honor—Honor Stevens.'

Honor Stevens. Verity felt her heart start to plummet with the sickening speed of an out-of-control lift. She was being stupid, of course. Stevens wasn't that unusual a name, and she was taking her own apprehension and coincidence too far to assume that just because of a shared surname that meant...

'Address?' the nurse asked crisply.

Dutifully Honor gave it.

'Parents?' she demanded.

'Parent. I only have one—my father,' Honor began weakly. 'His name's Silas. Well, really Silas Stevens.' She pulled a face and looked at Verity, and unexpectedly told her, 'You look…' She stopped, looked at her again speculatively, but Verity didn't notice.

Silas Stevens. Honor was Silas' daughter. Why on earth hadn't she known? Guessed? She could see so clearly now that the reason she had found Honor's features so oddly familiar was because she was Silas' daughter. She even had his thick, dark, unruly hair, for heaven's sake, and those long-lashed grey eyes—*they* were his, no doubts about it. That disconcertingly level look was his as well and…

'Are you feeling all right?'

Verity flushed as she realised that both Honor and the nurse were watching her.

'I'm fine,' she fibbed, adding dryly, 'but it isn't every day that I get an out-of-control roller blader courting death under my car wheels.'

And it certainly wasn't every day that she learned that that child was the daughter of a man…of *the* man… What would Honor think if she knew that once Verity had believed that Silas' children would be hers, that *she* would be the one to bear his babies, wear his ring, share his life…? But that had been before… Before her uncle had reminded her of where her real duty lay, and before Silas had told her so unequivocally that he had his own plans for his life and that they did not include playing second fiddle to another's wishes, another man's rules, another man's business.

'But I can't just walk away and leave him, leave *it*,' Verity had protested shakily when Silas had delivered an ultimatum to her. 'He needs me, Silas, he expects me to take over the business…'

'And what of my needs, my expectations?' Silas had asked her angrily.

In the end they had made up their quarrel, but six weeks later her uncle had announced that he had made arrangements for her to go to America where she would work for a firm manufacturing a similar range of medical equipment to their own, since he believed the experience would stand her in good stead when she took over his own business. She had been tempted to refuse, to rebel, but the strictness with which he had brought her up had stopped her—that and her sense of responsibility and duty towards not just him but the business as well. The twenty-year gap which had existed between him and her father, despite the fact that they had been brothers, had meant that her father himself had been a little in awe of him, and Verity, entering his household as a shy six-year-old suddenly bereft of her parents, had been too nervous, too despairingly unhappy over the loss of her mother and father, too intimidated to even think of rebelling against his stern dictatorship so that the seeds had been sown then for her to be taught by him to obey.

Later, away from his oppressive presence, she had started to mature into her own person, to feel able to make her own judgements and have her own values and she had known then, tried then…but it had been too late…

Quickly she veiled her eyes with her lashes just in case either Honor or the nurse might read what she was feeling.

'We'll need to take some X-rays and of course she'll have to see the doctor, although it doesn't look as though anything's wrong,' the nurse assured Verity.

'You'll wait here for me. You won't leave without me, will you?' Honor begged Verity as the nurse indicated that she was to follow her.

'I…' Verity hesitated. She too knew what it was like to feel alone, to feel abandoned, to feel that you had no one.

'Your father—' the nurse was beginning firmly, but Honor shook her head.

'No,' she said quickly. 'I don't want… He's away…on business and he won't be back un- til…until next week,' she responded.

The nurse was pursing her lips.

'Look, if it helps, I'll wait…and take full responsibility,' Verity offered.

'Well, I don't really know. It is most unorthodox,' the nurse began. 'Are you a relative, or—?'

'She's...she's going to be my new mother,' Honor cut in before Verity could say anything, and then looked pleadingly at her as the nurse looked questioningly at Verity, seeking confirmation of what she had just been told.

'I...I'll, er...I'll just wait here for you,' Verity responded, knowing that she ought by rights to have corrected Honor's outrageous untruth, but suspecting that there was more to the girl's fib than a mere desire to short-circuit officialdom and avoid waiting whilst the hospital contacted whoever it was that her father had left in official charge of her.

It baffled Verity that a parent—any parent, male or female—could be so grossly neglectful of their child's welfare, but she knew, of course, that it did happen, and one of the things she intended to do with her new-found wealth was to make sure that children in Honor's situation were not exposed to the kind of danger Honor had just suffered. What

Verity wanted to do was to establish a network of secure, outside-school, protective care for children whose parents for one reason or another simply could not be there for them. She knew that what she was taking on was a mammoth task, but she was determined and it was also one that was extremely dear to her heart.

It was almost an hour before the nurse returned with Honor, pronouncing briskly that she was fine.

'I'll run you home,' Verity offered as they walked back out into the early summer sunshine.

Honor had paused and was drawing a picture in the dust with the toe of her shoe.

'What is it? What's wrong?' Verity asked her.

'Er... Dad doesn't have to know about any of this, does he?' Honor asked her uncomfortably. 'It's just... Well...'

Verity watched her gravely for a few seconds, her heart going out to her, although she kept her feelings to herself as she told her qui-

etly, 'Well, *I'm* certainly not going to say anything to him.'

Wasn't that the truth? The thought of having
anything…*anything* whatsoever to do with
Silas Stevens was enough to bring her out in
a cold panic-induced sweat, despite the fact
that she would dearly have loved to have given
him a piece of her mind about his appalling
neglect of his daughter's welfare.

'You're not. That's great…' A huge smile
split Honor's face as she started to hurry towards Verity's car.

When they did get there, though, her face
fell a little as she saw the dent and scraped
paintwork where she had collided with the car.

'It's a BMW, isn't it? That means it's going
to be expensive to repair…'

'I'm afraid it does,' Verity agreed cordially.
She sternly refused to allow her mouth to
twitch into anything remotely suspicious of a
smile as Honor told her gravely, 'I *will* pay
you back for however much it costs, but it
could take an awfully long time. Dad's always
docking my pocket money,' she added with an

aggrieved expression. 'It isn't fair. He can be really mean...'

You too, Verity wanted to sympathise. She knew all about that kind of meanness. Her uncle had kept her very short of money when she'd been growing up, and even now she often found it difficult to spend money on herself without imagining his reaction—which was why her cupboards had been so bare of designer clothes and the car she had driven before kind-heartedness had driven her to purchase Charlotte's BMW had been a second-hand run-of-the-mill compact model.

'I get my spending money every week. I wanted to have a proper allowance but Dad says I'm still too young... Where do you live?' she asked Verity.

Calmly Verity told her, watching as she carefully memorised the address.

'Can you stop here?' Honor suddenly demanded urgently, adding, when Verity looked quizzically at her, 'I...I'd rather you didn't take me all the way home...just in case... well...'

'I won't take you all the way home,' Verity agreed, 'but I'm not going to stop until I can see that you get home safely from where I'm parked.'

To her relief Honor seemed to accept this ruling, allowing Verity to pull into the side of the road within eyesight of her drive.

'Will there be someone there?' Verity felt bound to ask her.

'Oh, yes,' Honor assured her sunnily. 'Anna will be there. Anna looks after me…us… She works for Dad at the garden centre when I'm at school… I won't forget about the money,' she promised Verity solemnly as she got out of the car.

'I'm sure you won't,' Verity agreed, equally seriously.

So Silas still had the garden centre.

She remembered how full of plans he had been for it when he had first managed to raise the money to buy it. Her uncle had been scornful of what Silas had planned to do.

'A gardener?' he had demanded when Verity had first told him about Silas' plans.

'You're dating a gardener? Where did you meet him?'

Verity could remember how her heart had sunk when she had been forced to admit that she had met Silas when he had come to do the gardens at the house. She had hung her head in shame and distress when her uncle had demanded to know what on earth she, with her background and her education, could possibly see in someone who mowed lawns for a living.

'It isn't like that,' Verity had protested, flying to the protection of her new-found love and her new-found lover. 'He's been to university but...'

'But what?' her uncle had demanded tersely.

'He...he found out when he was there that it wasn't what he wanted to do...'

'What university has taught me more than anything else,' Silas had told her, 'is to know myself, and what I know is that I would hate to be stuck in some stuffy office somewhere. I want to be in the fresh air, growing things... It's in my blood, after all. My great-grandfather was a gardener. He worked for the

Duke of Hartbourne as his head gardener. I don't *want* to work for someone else, though— I want to work for myself. I want to buy a plot of land, develop it, build a garden centre…'

Enthusiastically he had started to tell Verity all about his plans. Six years older than her, he had possessed a maturity, a masculinity, which had alternately enthralled and enticed her. He had represented everything that she had not had in her own life and she had fallen completely and utterly in love with him.

Automatically, she turned the car into the narrow road that led to the house originally owned by her uncle—the house where she had grown up; the house where she had first met Silas; the house where she had tearfully told him that her responsibility, her duty towards her uncle had to take precedence over their love. And so he had married someone else.

The someone else who must have been Honor's mother. He must have loved her a great deal not to have married for a second time. And he had quite obviously cherished her memory and his love for her far longer than he had cherished his much-proclaimed love for *her,* Verity acknowledged tiredly as she reached her destination and drove in through the ornate wrought-iron gates which were a new feature since she had lived in the house. Outwardly, though, in other ways, it remained very much the same. A large, turn-of-the-century house, of no particular aesthetic appeal or design.

Both her uncle and her father had spent their childhood in it but it had never, to Verity, seemed to be a family house, despite its size. Her uncle had changed very little in it since his own parents' death, and to Verity it had always possessed a dark, semi-brooding, solitary air, totally unlike the pretty warmth she remembered from the much smaller but far happier home she had shared with her parents.

After her return from America her uncle had sold the house. His own health had started to deteriorate, during Verity's absence, so he had set in motion arrangements to move the manufacturing side of the business to London. It had seemed to make good sense for both he and Verity to move there as well, Verity to her small mews house close to the river and her uncle to a comfortable apartment and the care of a devoted housekeeper.

Stopping her car, she reached into her handbag for the keys the letting agent had given her and then, taking a deep breath, she got out and headed for the house.

She wasn't really sure herself just why she had chosen to come back, not just to this house but to this town. There was, after all, nothing here for her, no one here for her.

Perhaps one of the reasons was to reassure herself that she *was* now her own person—that she had her own life; that she was finally free; that she had the right to make her own decision. She had done her duty to her uncle and to the business and now, at thirty-three, she stood on the threshold of a whole new way of life, even if she had not decided, as yet, quite what form or shape that life would take.

'What you need is a man...to fall in love,' Charlotte had teasingly advised her the previous summer when Verity had protested that it was impossible for her to take time off to go on holiday with her friend and her family. 'If you fell in love then you would have to find time…'

'Fall in love? Me? Don't be ridiculous,' Verity had chided her.

'Why not?' Charlotte had countered. 'Other people do—even other workaholics like you. You're an attractive, loving, lovable woman, Verity,' she had told her determinedly.

'Tell that to my shareholders,' Verity had joked, adding more seriously, 'I don't *need* any more complications in my life Charlie. I've already got enough and, besides, the men I get to meet aren't interested in the real me. They're only interested in the Verity Maitland who's the head of Maitland Medical…'

'Has there *ever* been anyone, Verity?' Charlotte had asked her gently. 'Any special someone…an old flame…?'

'No. No one,' Verity had lied, hardening her heart against the memories she'd been able to feel threatening to push past the barriers she had put in place against them.

She'd had her share of opportunities, of course—dates…men who had wanted to get to know her better—but…but she had never really been sure whether it had been her they had wanted or the business, and she had simply never cared enough to take the risk of finding out. She had already been hurt once by believing a man who had told her that he loved her. She wasn't going to allow it to happen a second time.

Squaring her shoulders, she inserted the key into the lock and turned the handle.

CHAPTER TWO

As SHE stepped into the house's long narrow hallway, Verity blinked in astonished surprise. Gone was the dark paint and equally dark carpet she remembered, the air of cold unwelcome and austere disapproval, and in their place the hallway glowed with soft warm colours, natural creams warmed by the sunlight pouring in through the window halfway up the stairs. The house felt different, she acknowledged.

Half an hour later, having subjected it to a thorough inspection, she had to admit that its present owners had done a wonderful job of transforming it. Her uncle would, of course, have been horrified both by the luxury and the total impracticality of the warm cream carpet that covered virtually every floor surface. Verity, on the other hand, found it both heartwarming and deliciously sensual, if one could

use such a word about something so mundane
as mere carpet. The bedroom carpet, for in-
stance, with its particularly thick and soft pile,
was so warm-looking that she had had to fight
an urge to slip off her shoes and curl her bare
toes into it. And as for the wonderful pseudo-
Victorian bathroom with its huge, deep tub and
luxurious fitments, not to mention the separate
shower room that went with it—it was a feast
for the eyes.

'It's the best we've got on our books,' the
agent had told her. 'The couple who own it
had it renovated to the highest standard and if
his company hadn't transferred him to
California they would still be living there
themselves.'

Well, at least she had plenty of wardrobe
space, Verity acknowledged a couple of hours
later, having lugged the last of her suitcases up
the stairs and started to remove their contents.

It had been Charlotte who had decided that
they should have a ceremonial clear-out of all
the plain, businesslike suits Verity had worn

during her years as Chief Executive and Chairperson of the company.

'Throw them out!'

Verity gasped in shock as she listened to what Charlotte was proposing.

'They're far too good for that. That cloth...'

'...will last forever. I know. I remember you telling me so when you originally ordered them—and that was five years ago.'

'Just after Uncle Toby died, yes, I know,' Verity agreed sombrely.

'I hated them on you then and they don't have any place in your life now,' Charlotte reminded her, adding, 'and, whilst we're on the subject, I just never, ever, want to see you wearing your hair up again—especially when it looks so wonderful down. Nature is very, very unfair,' she continued. 'Not only has she given you the most wonderful skin, a profile to die for and naturally navy blue eyes, she's also given you the most glorious honey-blonde hair. It's every bit as thick and gorgeous-looking as Cindy Crawford's and it curls naturally...'

'Cindy who?' Verity teased, laughing when Charlotte began to look appalled and holding her hands up in defeat as she admitted, 'It's okay. I do know who she is...'

'What *you* need to do is to cultivate a more natural, approachable look,' Charlotte counselled her. 'Think jeans and white tees, a navy blazer and loafers, with your hair left down and just a smidgen of make-up.'

'Charlie,' Verity warned, telling her friend, 'I've been in business far too long not to recognise someone trying to package an item for sale.'

'The only person *you* need selling to is yourself,' Charlotte countered. 'I've lost count of the number of men I've introduced you to who you've simply frozen out... One day you're going to wake up on your own heading for forty and—'

'Is that such a very bad deal?' Verity objected.

'Well, there *are* other things in life,' Charlotte reminded her, 'and I've watched you often enough with my two to know how good you are with children.'

It wasn't a subject which Verity wanted to pursue. Not even Charlie, who was arguably her closest friend, knew about Silas and the pain he had caused her, the hopes she had once had...the love she had once given him, only to have it thrown back in her face when he had married someone else, despite telling her... But what was the point in going back over old ground?

She had been nineteen when she and Silas had first met; twenty-two when he had married—someone else—and what time they had had together had been snatched between her years at university, followed by a brief halcyon period of less than six months between her finishing university and being sent to America by her uncle. Halcyon to her, that was. For Silas?

Face it, she told herself sternly now as she hung the last of her spectacular new clothes into the wardrobe. He was never really serious about you, despite everything he said. If he had been he'd have done as he promised.

'I'll love you forever,' he had told her the first time they had made love. 'You're everything I've ever wanted, everything I *will* ever want…'

But he had been lying to her, Verity acknowledged dry-eyed. He had never really loved her at all. And why on earth he had encouraged her to believe that he did, she really could not understand. He had never struck her as the kind of man who needed the ego-boost of making sexual conquests. He was tall, brown-haired and grey-eyed, with the kind of physique that came from working hard out of doors, and Verity had fallen in love with him without needing any encouragement or coaxing. She had just finished her first year at university and come home for the holidays to find him working in her uncle's garden. He had introduced himself to her and had watched her quizzically as she had been too inexperienced, too besotted, to hide her immediate reaction to him, her face and her body blushing a deep vivid pink.

Verity tensed, remembering just how betrayingly her over-sensitive young body *had* revealed her reaction to him, her nipples underneath the thin tee shirt she had been wearing hardening so that she had instinctively crossed her arms over her breasts to hide their flaunting wantonness. He, Silas, had affected not to notice what had happened to her or how embarrassed she had been by it, tactfully turning his head and gently directing her attention to the flower bed he had been weeding, making some easy, relaxed comment about the design of the garden, giving her time to recover her equilibrium and yet, somehow, at the same time, closing the distance between them so that when he'd started to draw her attention to another part of the garden he'd been close enough to her to be able to touch her bare arm with his hand.

Verity could remember even now how violently she had quivered in immediate reaction to his touch.

Fatefully she had turned her head to look at him, her wide-eyed gaze going first to his eyes and then helplessly to his mouth.

He had told her later that the only thing that had stopped him from snatching her up and kissing her there and then had been his fear of frightening her away.

'You looked so young and innocent that I was afraid you might... I was afraid that if I let you see just how much I wanted you, I'd frighten you, terrify the life out of you,' he had told her rawly, weeks later, as he'd held her in his arms and kissed her over and over again, the way she had secretly wanted him to and equally secretly been afraid that he might that first day in the garden.

Looking back with the maturity she had since gained, she could still see no signs, no warnings of what was to be or the full enormity of how badly she was going to be hurt.

She had believed Silas implicitly when he had told her that he loved her. Why should she not have done? *He*, after all, had been the one who had pursued her, courted her, laid seige to her heart and her emotions, her life.

That first summer had been a brilliant kaleidoscope of warmth, love and laughter, or so it seemed looking back on it. She had still been talking to Silas hours later when her uncle had returned home, her bags still standing on the drive where the taxi driver had dropped them and her off. She had been blissfully unaware of just how late it had been until she'd seen her uncle draw up.

'Still here?' he asked Silas curtly, nodding dismissively to him as he turned to Verity and demanded frowningly, 'I should have thought you'd have too much studying to do to waste your time out here, Verity…'

Chastened, Verity bade Silas a mumbled 'goodbye' and turned to follow her uncle into the house. But when she went to pick up her bags, Silas had got there first, gathering up the two heaviest cases as though they weighed a mere nothing.

To Verity, used as she was to the far more frail frame of her elderly uncle, the sight of so much raw, sexual, male strength was dizzyingly exciting.

Her uncle lectured her over supper about the need for her to allocate time during her summer vacation for working hard at her studies.

'Of course, you'll come to the factory with me during the day,' he informed her, and Verity did not attempt to argue. Every holiday since she had turned sixteen had been spent thus, with her learning every aspect of the business from the factory floor upwards, under her uncle's critical eye.

But fate, it seemed, had had other plans for her. The following morning when she went downstairs—her uncle always insisted on leaving for the factory well before seven so that he could be there before the first workers arrived at eight—she learned that her uncle had received a telephone call late the previous evening informing him that the firm's Sales Director had been taken to hospital with acute appendicitis, which meant that her uncle was going to have to step into his shoes and fly to the Middle East to head a sales delegation.

He would, he informed Verity, be gone for almost a month.

'I shall have to leave you here to your own devices,' he told her. 'I can't have you going into the factory without my supervision. Had this happened a little earlier I could have made arrangements for you to come with me. It would have been excellent experience for you but, unfortunately, it's far too late now for you to have the necessary inoculations and for me to get a visa for you. Still, you must have brought work home with you from university.'

'Yes,' she agreed meekly, eyes downcast, her heart suddenly bounding so frantically fast against her chest wall that she felt positively light-headed.

Even with her uncle gone she was still unable to acknowledge the real reason for her excitement and sense of freedom, nor for her sudden decision to work in the sitting room which overlooked the part of the garden which Silas had been working on the previous day and to wear a pair of cotton shorts which showed off her long slim legs.

Silas arrived within an hour of her uncle's departure, and from her strategic position in the sitting room Verity was able to discreetly watch him as he worked. As the day grew hotter he stopped working and stood up, stretching his back before removing his soft cotton tee shirt.

Dry-mouthed, Verity watched him, her body shaking with the most disturbing sensation she had ever experienced.

'Lust,' she told herself angrily now as she folded the last few pairs of briefs and put them neatly into one of the wardrobe drawers.

Lust: she had been too naive to know just what that was or how powerful it could be *then*. All she *had* known was that, no matter how hard she tried to concentrate on her work and the words on the paper in front of her, all that she could really see was Silas' image imprinted on her eyeball.

At lunch time she had gone outside to offer him a cold drink and something to eat. Gravely he had accepted, following her into the kitchen, and it had only been later that he had admitted to her that he had brought his own refreshments with him but that the opportunity to spend some time with her had been too much of a temptation for him to resist.

Over the light salad lunch she had quickly and nervously prepared for him—Verity had possessed very few domestic skills in those days; her uncle had considered that learning them was a waste of time when she was going to take over his business and they had a housekeeper who lived in, but who fortuitously was away at that time taking her annual period of leave—Verity had listened wide-eyed whilst Silas had described to her his work and his plans.

'That's enough about me,' he announced gruffly when they had both finished eating. 'What about you? What do you intend to do with your life?'

'Me? I'm going to take over my uncle's business,' Verity told him gravely. 'That's what he's training me for. I'm the only person he's got to inherit it, you see. It's his life's work and—'

'*His* life's work, but *you* have your own life and the right to make your own choices, surely?' Silas interrupted her sharply, before telling her pointedly, '*My* parents originally wanted me to train as a doctor like my father, but they would never impose that kind of decision on me, nor would I allow them to...'

'I...my uncle... My uncle took me in when my parents were killed,' Verity explained low-voiced to him. 'I've always known that he expects me...that he wants me... I'm very lucky, really, it's a wonderful opportunity...'

'It's a wonderful opportunity if it's what you really want,' Silas agreed, 'otherwise it's... *Is* it what you want, Verity?'

'I... I... It's what's expected of me,' Verity told him a little unsteadily. It was proving virtually impossible to concentrate on what he was saying with him sitting so close to her—close enough for her to be intensely, embarrassingly aware of his body and its evident physical masculinity, its tantalising male scent. He had asked her permission to 'clean up' before sitting down to lunch with her and his discarded shirt was now back on.

Every time she dared to look at him she was swept with such an intense and heightened awareness of him that she could feel her face starting to flush with hot self-consciousness.

'What's *expected* of you? Listen,' Silas commanded her, reaching out and taking hold of her hand, keeping it between his own with an open easiness which robbed her of the ability to object or protest. 'No one has the right to *expect* anything of you. *You* have the right to choose for yourself what you do with your life. It is *your* life you're living you know, and not your uncle's...'

Verity bit her lip.

'I... I know,' she responded uncertainly, 'but...'

'I'm having a day off tomorrow,' Silas told her, changing the subject. 'There's a garden that's open to the public twenty miles away— I was planning to go and see it. Would you like to come with me?'

Shiny-eyed and flushed with delighted happiness, Verity nodded.

'Good,' he told her. 'I'll pick you up at nine, if that's okay.'

Once again Verity nodded, not trusting herself to speak.

Silas was still holding her hand and she had to tug it before he released it, giving her a rueful smile as he did so.

Of course, she didn't do any work for the rest of the day, nor did she sleep that night.

Three outfits were tried on and discarded before Silas arrived to pick her up, and she blushed betrayingly at the appraising look he gave her as he studied her jeans-clad figure and the neat way the denim hugged her small firm bottom.

Jeans. How long had it been since she had worn a pair of those? Verity wondered grimly now, as the rest of her underwear joined the items she had already put away.

She had acquired a couple of pairs from Charlotte, designer labelled and immaculately tailored.

'You could have taken these with you,' Verity had protested when Charlotte had handed them over to her.

'What? Wear Lauren where *we're* going? Do you mind? The jeans *I'll* be wearing now are a pair of sturdy 501s,' she had told Verity, her face breaking into a wide grin as she had caught sight of the raised-eyebrowed look her friend had been giving her.

'Oh, 501s. Poor you,' Verity had commented dryly.

'Well, they might be ''in'' fashion-wise but they are also ideally designed for working in and, besides, the Lauren ones are too tight. I can barely move in them. They'll fit you much better—you're slimmer than I am right now.'

Jeans. Verity went to the wardrobe and pulled them out, touching the fabric exploratively, smoothing it beneath her fingertips.

The jeans she had worn on that first date with Silas had been a pair she had bought from her allowance. Thus far, she had not worn them in front of her uncle, knowing that he would not have approved. He had been a rather old-fashioned man who had not liked to see women wearing 'trousers'—of any kind.

Courteously Silas had held the door open for her on the passenger side of his small pick-up. The inside of the vehicle had been spotlessly clean, Verity had noticed, just as she had noticed that Silas was a good and considerate driver.

The gardens they had gone to see had been spectacularly beautiful, she acknowledged, but she had to admit that she had not paid as much attention as she ought to have done to them, nor to Silas' explanation of how the borders had been planted and the colour combinations in them constructed. She had been far too busy studying how he was constructed, far too busy noticing just how wonderfully dedicated to her task nature had been when she had put *him* together with such spectacular sensuality. Even the way he'd walked had made her heart lurch against her ribs, and just to look at his mouth, never mind imagining how it might feel to be kissed by it…by him…

'What's wrong? Are you feeling okay?' Silas asked her at one point.

'I'm fine,' Verity managed to croak, petrified of him guessing what she was really feeling.

He had brought them both a packed lunch—far more tasty and enjoyable than the meal *she* had prepared for him the previous day, Verity acknowledged, assuming, until he told her otherwise, that his mother had prepared it for them.

'Ma? No way,' he told her. 'She believes in us all being self-sufficient and, besides, she works—she's a nurse. My two brothers are both married now and I'm the only one left at home, but Ma still insists on me making my own packed lunches. One thing she did teach us all as a nurse, though, was the importance of good nutrition. Take these sandwiches. They're on wholemeal bread with a low-fat spread, the tuna provides very important nutrients and the salad I've put with it is good and healthy.'

'Like these,' Verity teased him, waving in front of him the two chocolate bars he had packed.

Silas laughed.

'Chocolate *is* good for you,' he told her solemnly, adding with a wicked smile, 'It's the food of love, did you know that…?'

'Want me to prove it?' he tempted when Verity shook her head.

He enjoyed teasing her, he admitted later, but what he enjoyed even more, he added, was the discovery that beneath her shyness she possessed not just intelligence but, even more importantly, a good sense of humour.

They certainly laughed a lot together that first summer; laughed a lot and loved a lot too.

She could still remember the first time he kissed her. It wasn't sunny that day. There was thunder in the air, the sky brassy and overcast, and then late in the afternoon it suddenly came on to rain, huge, pelting drops, causing them to take refuge in the small summer house several yards away at the bottom of the garden.

They ran there, Silas holding her hand, both of them bursting into the small, stuffy room, out of breath and laughing.

As the door swung closed behind them, enclosing them in the half-light of the small, airless room, Silas turned towards her, brushing her hair off her face. His hands were cool and wet and, without thinking what she was doing, she turned her head to lick a raindrop off him, an instinctive, almost childish gesture, but one which marked the end of her childhood, turning her within the space of an afternoon from a child to a woman.

Even without closing her eyes she could still visualise the expression in Silas' eyes, feel the tension that suddenly gripped his body. Outwardly, nothing had changed. He was still cupping her face, they were still standing with their bodies apart, but inwardly *everything* had changed, Verity acknowledged.

Looking into Silas' eyes, she felt herself starting to tremble—not with cold and certainly not with fear.

'Verity.'

Her name, which Silas started saying inches from her face, he finished mouthing with his lips against her own, his *body* against her own.

And there was nothing remotely childish about the way she reached out to him—for him—Verity remembered; nothing remotely childish at all in the way she opened her mouth beneath his and deliberately invited him to explore its intimacy. They kissed frantically, feverishly, whispering incomprehensible words of love and praise to one another, she making small keening sounds of pleasure against Silas' skin, he muttering rawly to her that he loved her, adored her, wanted her. Over and over again they kissed and touched and Verity felt incandescent with the joy of what she was experiencing; of being loved; of knowing that Silas loved her as much as she knew she loved him.

They weren't lovers that day. She wanted to but Silas shook his head, telling her huskily, 'We can't... I can't... I don't have... I could make you pregnant,' he explained to her, adding gruffly, 'The truth is I would *want* to make you pregnant, Verity. That's how much I love you and I know that once I had you in my arms, once my body was inside yours, there's no way I could... I want to come inside you,' he told her openly when she looked uncertainly at him, explaining in a low, emotional voice, 'I want to have that kind of intimacy with you. It's man's most basic instinct to regenerate himself, to seed the fertility of his woman, especially when he loves her as much as I love you.'

'I... I could go on the pill...' Verity offered, but Silas shook his head.

'No,' he told her gently, 'taking care of that side of things is *my* responsibility. And besides,' he continued softly, looking around the cramped, stuffy summer house, 'this isn't really the right place. When you and I make love I want it to be...I want it to be special for you...perfect.'

Verity moistened her lips.

'My uncle is still away,' she offered awkwardly. 'We could...'

'No. Not here in another man's house. Yes, I know that it's your home, but no, not here,' Silas said quietly.

'Where, then?' Verity breathed eagerly.

'Leave it to me,' Silas told her. 'Leave everything to me...'

And like the dutiful person she had been raised to be she dipped her head and agreed.

CHAPTER THREE

THE doorbell rang just as Verity had finished her unpacking. Frowning, she went downstairs to answer it. Who on earth could that be? She certainly wasn't expecting anyone.

She was still frowning when she opened the door, a small gasp of shock escaping her lips as she saw who was standing there and recognised him immediately.

'Silas!'

Instinctively her hand went to her throat as she tried, too late, to suppress that betraying whisper of sound.

'Verity,' her visitor responded grimly. 'May I come in?'

Without waiting for her assent he was shouldering his way into the hallway.

'How…how did you know I was back?' Verity managed to ask him huskily. Was it possible that he had actually grown taller *and* broader in the years they had been apart? Surely not, and yet she couldn't remember him ever filling the space of the hallway quite so imposingly before. He might be over ten years older but he was *still* as magnetically male as she remembered, she recognised unwillingly, and perhaps even more so—as a young man he had worn his sexuality very carelessly, softening it with the tenderness and consideration he had shown her.

Now... She took a deep breath and tried to steady her jittery nerves. Now there was *nothing* remotely soft nor tender about the way he was looking at her. Far from it.

'I didn't until I did a check at the hospital and found out that *you* had accompanied Honor there. What the hell kind of person *are* you, Verity? First you damn near run my daughter over and then you don't even bother to let *me* know that she's had an accident. What am I saying? I know *exactly* what kind of woman you are, don't I? Why should I be surprised at *anything* you might choose to do, after all I know?'

Verity couldn't utter a word. What was he saying? What was he trying to accuse her of doing? She... He made it sound as though she had deliberately tried to hit Honor, when the truth was...

'I did what I thought was best,' she told him coolly. There was no way she was going to let him see just how much he had caught her off guard, or how agitated and ill-equipped to deal with him she actually felt.

Thinking about him earlier had done nothing to prepare her for the reality of him. She had been thinking about, remembering, a young man in his twenties. *This* was a mature adult male in his late thirties and a man who...

'What *you* thought was best?' He gave her an incredulously angry look as he repeated her words. 'Didn't it strike you that as Honor's father *I* had the right to know what had happened? Didn't it cross that cold little mind of yours that *you* had a responsibility to let me know what had happened? After all, you used to be very big on responsibility, didn't you? Oh, but I was forgetting, the kind of respon-

sibility you favoured was the kind that
meant—'

'I didn't get in touch with you because I had
no idea that you were Honor's father until we
got to the hospital,' Verity interrupted him
quickly, 'and by then...'

By then Honor had begged her not to let her
father know what had happened and, addition-
ally, untruthfully told both her and the nurse
that Silas was unavailable and out of the country. But she certainly wasn't going to tell Silas
that. Against all the odds, and ridiculously, she
felt a certain sense of kinship, of female bonding with Honor.

Female *bonding* with a *ten*-year-old? And
she was supposed to be intelligent? Charlotte
was right—she *did* need to get a grip on her
life.

'Presumably, though, you knew by the time
Honor had informed the nurse that *you* were
going to be her stepmother,' he informed her
with deadly acidness.

She was surely far too old and had far too
much self-control to be betrayed now by the

kind of hot-faced blush which had betrayed her so readily all those years ago, but nonetheless Verity found herself hurriedly looking away from the anger she could see in Silas' eyes and curling her toes into her shoes as she fibbed, 'Uh...did she...? I really don't remember... the casualty department was busy,' she embroidered. 'I just wanted to make sure that Honor got some medical attention—'

'Liar.' Silas cut across her stumbled explanation in a brutally incisive voice that made her wince. 'And don't think I don't know *exactly* why you laid claim to a non-existent relationship between us.'

This was worse than her worst possible nightmare, worse by far than the most embarrassing and humiliating thing she could ever have imagined happening to her, Verity decided. She could *never* remember feeling so exposed and vulnerable, so horribly conscious of having her deepest and most private emotions laid bare to be derided and scorned. No, not even the first time she had had to stand up in front of her late uncle's board of directors, knowing how much each and every one of them must secretly have been resenting her appointment as their leader, as the person to whom they would have to defer.

In that one sentence Silas had torn down, trampled, flattened, all the delicate defences she had worked so hard to weave together to protect herself with—defences she had created with patience and teeth-gritting determination; defences she had bonded together with good humour and cheerful smiles, determined never to allow *anyone* to guess what she was really feeling, or to guess how empty her life sometimes felt, how far short of her once idealistic expectations it had fallen. Other people's compassion and pity were something she had always shrunk from and gently rejected. Her lack of a man to share her life, a child to share her love—these had been things she had determinedly told herself she was not going to allow herself to yearn for. She had her *life*, her *friends*, her *health*.

But now, pitilessly and brutally, Silas had destroyed that precious, fragile peace of mind she had worked with gentle determination to achieve.

Silas had guessed, unearthed, exhumed the pitiful little secret she had so safely hidden from other eyes.

Bravely Verity lifted her head. She wasn't going to let him have a *total* victory. Something could be salvaged from the wreckage, the destruction he had caused, even if it was only her pride.

'Contrary to what you seem to think—' she began, but once again Silas wouldn't let her finish.

He cut her off with a furious, 'I don't *think*. I *know*. You let the nurse believe that you had the right to sign Honor's consent form because you thought it would get you off the hook, that that way you wouldn't have to face up to what you had done, nor suffer any potential legal consequences.

'My God, what kind of woman are you to be driving so carelessly in a built-up area in the first place, and at school-leaving time? But, then, we both already know the answer to that, don't we? Such mundane matters as children's safety, children's lives, simply don't matter to you, do they? You've got far more important things to concern yourself with. How many millions are you worth these days, Verity? No doubt that car outside is just *one* of the perks that comes with being a very rich woman.

'Funny—I knew, of course, that the business came first, second and third with you, but I never had you down as a woman who needed to surround herself with all the trappings of a materialistic lifestyle.'

Verity gave him a dazed, almost semi-blind look. What was he saying—something about her car? About her wealth? It didn't matter. All that mattered was the intense feeling of relief she felt on realising that he hadn't, after all, meant what she had thought he had meant by that comment about knowing why she had not refuted Honor's outrageous claim that she was soon to become her stepmother. That he had thought she had allowed his daughter's fib to stand so that no questions could be asked about the accident, not because secretly she still yearned for...still wanted...

'My God, but you've changed,' she heard him breathing angrily. 'That car...this house... those clothes...'

Her clothes... Verity pushed aside her euphoric sense of relief—there would be time for her to luxuriate in that later when she was on her own.

'I'm wearing jeans,' she managed to point out in quiet self-defence.

'Designer jeans,' Silas told her curtly, nodding in the direction of the logo sewn on them.

Designer jeans? How had Silas known that? The Silas she remembered simply wouldn't have known or cared where her clothes had come from. The Silas *she* knew and remembered would, in fact, have been far more interested in what lay beneath her clothes rather than the name of the design house they had originated from.

Quickly, Verity redirected her thoughts, telling him dryly what her own quick eye had already noticed.

'Your own clothes are hardly basic chain store stuff.'

Was that just a hint of betraying caught-out colour seeping up under his skin? Verity wondered triumphantly.

'I didn't choose them,' he told her stiffly.

Then who had? A woman? For some reason his admission took all her original pleasure at catching him out away from her, Verity acknowledged dismally.

'I suppose you thought you were being pretty clever and that you'd got away with damn near killing my daughter,' Silas was demanding to know, back on the attack again. 'Well, unfortunately for you a...a friend of mine just happened to see you at the scene of the accident and she took a note of your car's registration number.'

'Really? How very neighbourly of her,' Verity gritted. 'I don't suppose it occurred to her that she might have been more usefully employed trying to help Honor rather than playing at amateur detective?'

'Myra was on her way to a very important meeting. She's on the board of several local charities and, as she said, she could hardly expect busy business people who are already giving their time to feel inclined to make a generous cash donation to a charity when its chairperson can't even be on time for a meeting...'

Whoever this Myra was, Silas obviously thought an awful lot of her, Verity reflected. He made her sound like a positive angel.

'You aren't going to deny that you *were* responsible for Honor's accident, I hope?' Silas continued, returning to the attack.

Verity was beginning to get angry herself now. How dared he speak to her like this? Would he have done so had he not already known her, judged her...had she been a stranger? Somehow she doubted it. He was being unfairly critical of her, unfairly caustic towards her because of who she was, because once she had been foolish enough to love him, and he had been— Quickly she gathered up her dangerously out-of-control thoughts.

Deny that she was responsible? But she
hadn't been responsible. It was… On the point
of opening her mouth to vigorously inform
him just how wrong he was, Verity abruptly
remembered her conversation with Honor and
the little girl's anxiety. Quickly she closed it
again.

'It *was* an *accident*,' was all she could per-
mit herself to say.

'An accident caused by the fact that *you*
were driving too selfishly and too fast along a
suburban road, in a car more properly designed
for fast driving on an *autobahn*, or in your
case, probably more truthfully, for showing off
amongst your friends.'

Verity gasped.

'For your information,' she began, 'I bought
that car…' On the point of telling him just why
she had bought the BMW, she suddenly
changed her mind. After all, what explanations
did she possibly owe *him*? None. None at all.

'I bought that car because I wanted to buy
it—because I liked it. No doubt your *friend*
prefers to drive something ecologically sound,

modest and economical. She has a Beetle, perhaps, or maybe a carefully looked after Morris Minor which she inherited from some aged aunt...' she suggested acidly.

'As a matter of fact—not that it's any business of yours, Myra drives a Jaguar. It was part of the settlement she received when she divorced her husband... But I'm not here to talk about my friends or my private life. You do realise, don't you, that I could report you to the police for dangerous driving?'

Immediately Verity froze, unable to control her expression.

'Yes, you may well look shocked,' Silas told her grimly.

'You can't do that,' Verity protested, thinking of Honor.

'Can't I? I've certainly got a damned good mind to, although, given your cavalier attitude towards the truth and the fact that there were no witnesses to the *whole* event, no doubt you'd manage to find a way of extricating yourself.'

'*Me* cavalier with the truth? That's rich coming from you,' Verity retorted bitterly.

'What the hell do you mean by that?' Silas challenged her.

Verity glared at him, her own temper as hot as his now. After all, she could hardly remind him that he had once told her he loved her; that he would always love her; that there would never be anyone else.

'Why have you come back here?' he demanded abruptly.

Verity turned her face away from him so that he couldn't fully see her expression.

'I grew up here. It's my home town,' she reminded him quietly.

'Sentiment. You've come back out of sentiment. My God, now I really have heard everything!'

'My roots are here,' Verity continued, praying that nothing in her voice or her expression would reveal to him how very, very much his cruelty was hurting her.

'Roots, maybe,' Silas allowed in a biting voice. 'But if you're hoping to revisit the past or resurrect old—'

'I'm not hoping to do any such thing,' Verity interrupted him passionately. 'So far as I'm concerned, the past is the past and that's exactly how I intend it to stay. There's *nothing* in it that I miss.'

'Nothing in it that you miss and certainly nothing in it that you ever valued,' Silas agreed.

And then to Verity's shock he suddenly took a step towards her.

'Silas.' Dizzily Verity moved too, but not back away from him putting more distance between them as she had planned. No. Instead what she actually did was take a step towards him. A step that brought her within intimate reach of his body, within his private body space, and close enough to him not just to see the dark shadowing along his jaw where his beard would grow but also to reach out and touch it, to feel it prickling against her palm as she had done all those years ago, the first time they had shared a bed together, and she had woken up in the opalescent light of a summer morning in the euphoric knowledge that

he was there beside her, that she had the bliss-
ful, awesome right to simply turn her head and
watch him as he slept, knowing that he was
hers; that *she* was his, that nothing and no one
could cause them to part—ever.

Silas!

Verity closed her eyes. She could feel the
deep, uneven, heavy thud thud of her own
heartbeat, pounding through her body in urgent
summons. Was it *that* that was making her feel
so weak, so…?

'I'm warning you, Verity, stay away from
me. Stay out of my life…'

The ugly words hit her like blows aimed vi-
ciously into her unprotected vulnerable emotions. Instinctively she tried to protect herself
from them by wrapping her arms around her
body, but Silas was already turning away from
her and heading for the door.

'I mean it,' he warned her as he paused to
open it. 'Stay out of my life.'

She must be suffering some kind of shock,
Verity decided dazedly ten minutes later as she
slowly made her way back upstairs.

Stay out of *his* life? Did he *really* think he needed to warn her off, that she didn't *know* that there was no place there for her, no love there for her?

Numbly she stared out of her bedroom window and into the garden below. From this window she could just about see the roof of the little summer house where they had sheltered from the rain, and it had been here in this room, if not on this bed, that she had lain dreaming her foolish, idealistic, heated, adoring, loving, girlish dreams of him.

And it had been here too that she had lain in the days after he had fully made love to her, feeling and believing that the reality of his lovemaking had far, far outstripped even her most feverish and sensually exciting daydreams.

It had been here too in this room, this sanctuary, that she had come after that dreadful quarrel when he had challenged her to choose between her love for him and her duty to her uncle, and here too that she had cried her tears of relief and happiness when he had told her,

with remorse and regret, that the last thing he
had wanted to do was to hurt her; that hurting
her had hurt him even more and that, of course,
he had understood that she had to at least attempt, as a matter of duty and honour, to ac-
cede to her uncle's wishes.

'It won't be for long,' she had promised him
as he had held her face and her tears had
flowed down onto his hands. 'America isn't
really so very far away and when I come
back…'

'When you come back I'm never ever going
to let you out of my sight again,' he had told
her savagely. 'If you weren't so damned stub-
born I wouldn't be letting you go now.'

'I have to go,' she had wept. 'I owe it to my
uncle…' And yet she had known even as she
had said the words that a part of her had
longed for him to snatch her away, to refuse
to allow her to leave him, to, however implau-
sible it would have been, insist.

'You could come with me,' she had even
suggested. 'You could work over there…'

'Come with you? As what?' He had balked immediately, telling her, 'I'm a independent man, Verity. I *can't* live on your coat tails and, besides, what about our plans to buy the small holding we visited last week—to develop the garden centre...?

Verity closed her eyes now and leant her hot face against the cool glass.

'I'll wait for you,' he had promised her when she had left. 'I'll wait for you, no matter how long it takes...'

Only he hadn't...he hadn't waited. Hadn't loved her. Hadn't given her the wedding ring nor the child he had promised her so passionately and, she had believed, so meaningfully.

Oh, God! Had he guessed just now in the hallway, when she had stepped towards him instead of stepping away, just what was going through her mind, her body? How *easy* it would have been for her to...? Had he known that a foolish, idiotic part of her had actually thought that he *was* going to kiss her, that he had *wanted* to kiss her? That that same foolish, idiotic part of her remembered with such aching intensity that that was exactly how he used to move towards her when…?

'No,' Verity protested despairingly beneath her breath. 'No…please, no…' But it was already too late, already the memories were flooding back, swamping her. The first time he had made love to her… She could remember it as clearly and intensely as though it had only happened yesterday.

They had been out together for the day. Another visit to a famous garden—Silas, as she had discovered by this time, was a passionate advocate of the importance of good garden structure.

'Not having a proper structure to me is like…like…well, imagine trying to clothe a human body if all the limbs had simply been stuck on haphazardly here and there and everywhere, or if a house had been designed simply by adding one room next to another…'

And he produced books and then drawings to show Verity to reinforce his point. Completely head over heels in love with him by this stage, Verity acknowledged that she

was probably spending longer gazing ador-
ingly at the way his hair curled into his collar
and flopped over his forehead than studying
the designs he was showing her, but she took
on board all that he was saying and she was
as impressed and excited as he was by the elegant simplicity of the gardens they went to
see.

'Every garden has a right to be properly designed,' he told her passionately, 'and you
only have to read one of Sir Roy Strong's
books to see just how the concept of good architectural design can be transferred to even
the smallest urban garden.'

They were sitting eating their sandwiches at
the time.

'Mmm…' Verity agreed, smiling lovingly at
him.

And then he put down his sandwich and removed hers from her, and took her in his arms
and kissed her lingeringly and very, very thoroughly, but very gently, before lifting his head
and looking from her love-dazed eyes to her
kiss softened mouth before telling her rawly,

'You don't know what I'd give right now to be somewhere alone with you and private...'

Very slowly he reached out and traced the shape of her lips with his fingertip.

'Perfect,' he whispered tenderly.

'Good architectural design,' Verity whispered teasingly back.

'Better than that. The best,' Silas told her solemnly, but then the laughter died out of his eyes as the tip of his finger touched the centre of her bottom lip and Verity could feel it and him starting to shake with need—a need which she fully reciprocated.

'Couldn't we do that—be together?' Verity asked him huskily.

They talked about becoming lovers but Silas told her that he had applied the brakes to his plans to find them the perfect hideaway because he wanted to wait until he was sure it was what she wanted—he was what she wanted—and that he didn't want to rush her.

'We could...there's my bedroom,' Verity boldly offered her home again. Her uncle was away on another trip. The Sales Director's appendicitis had proved more problematic than his doctors had first expected, causing a delay in his recovery, and her uncle had had to take over his duties and was consequently away on business far more than usual.

'No, not there,' Silas answered firmly, 'but if you're sure…'

His hand was holding the back of her head, caressing her scalp through her hair. Shivering with excitement and emotion, Verity smiled tremulously at him. The look in his eyes made her face burn—and not with the embarrassment of coy self-consciousness of a young woman who was still a virgin.

'I'm sure,' she told him positively. 'Oh, Silas, I'm so sure…'

'I want everything to be right—special,' he told her gruffly. 'I've looked into some of the hotels in the area and I could book us a room—for tonight…'

'Oh, yes, yes,' Verity breathed.

Tenderly she reached out and touched his face, feeling the warmth of his skin beneath her fingertips, the hard firmness of the bones

and muscles that lay below it. She might not
have been physically experienced, might never
have had a previous lover, but she had no
sense of fear nor trepidation, simply a deep
inner knowledge of how right this was, of how
right Silas was!

Silas found them a hotel several miles away
from the garden they had visited. Small and
privately owned, it was set in its own gardens
but, for once, after they had booked in, Silas
showed no inclination to explore.

'I…I thought you might like to…to see the
gardens,' Verity had protested a little uncertainly once they were alone in the room.

Silas shook his head quietly, locking the
door before turning back to her.

'No. Right now there's only one thing I
want to do, one garden I want to explore,' he
said softly, and Verity knew from the way he
looked at her, his glance slowly caressing
every inch of her, just exactly what he meant.

'I…what…? I don't know what to do,' she
told him finally and honestly, blushing and

then laughing. 'Well, I do, at least I think I do, but...'

'Come here,' Silas commanded her and, her colour still high, Verity walked unsteadily into his arms.

They had kissed before of course, and touched intimately so, but never like this, Verity acknowledged as Silas kissed his way slowly along the soft line of her lips and then, repeating the gesture he had made earlier, pressed the pad of his thumb to the centre of her bottom lip, hungrily nibbling the tender flesh he had exposed, his arms tightening possessively around her as Verity trembled in response to his touch. His tongue slowly caressed the inner sweetness of her mouth as hers did his and then he slowly and rhythmically sucked on her tongue and taught her to do the same to his.

As she repeated his sensual, intimate caress, Verity could feel the jolt that ran through his body and the sexual hardening and arousal that went with it.

Wrapping her arms around him, she pressed herself just as close to him as she could get, instinctively rubbing her body lovingly against his and making little purring sounds of pleasure as she did so, her eyes closing.

'Verity, Verity,' she heard Silas groaning as his hands gripped her waist half as though he was going to put her slightly away from him, but then he changed his mind, his hands sliding down her body to cup her buttocks and grind his own hips into her receptive body.

A delicious shiver of pleasure convulsed her and Silas removed one of his hands from her bottom to gently rub and knead the length of her spine in a caress that was so tenderly soothing that it made Verity open her eyes and look dazedly up at him.

'I don't want to take things too fast,' Silas told her rawly in response to her unspoken question. 'This will be your first time and I want...I want to make it perfect for you—in every way, Verity.'

'It will be,' she promised him, knowing as she spoke the words that they were true, with some deep rooted primal feminine wisdom that didn't need to be analysed or questioned.

Gently and lovingly, Silas undressed her, pausing to caress and kiss each bit of flesh he exposed, but once he got to her breasts, Verity felt his self-control beginning to slip away. As he slowly circled one taut, hard, flushed nipple with the pad of his thumb she knew it wasn't just her who was trembling so violently in sensual reaction.

'These are the most beautiful…you are the most perfect thing I have ever seen,' he whispered throatily as he picked her up and carried her over to the huge king-sized bed.

'More perfect than one of Sir Roy Strong's gardens,' Verity teased him remembering their earlier shared humour.

An answering smile crinkled the corners of his mouth and momentarily lightened the passion that had darkened his eyes as he teased back, 'Who's Sir Roy Strong?'

Their laughter immediately banished whatever small feeling of self-consciousness Verity felt she might otherwise have had and very

soon her fingers were equally busy as Silas',
if not perhaps quite as patient, as she tugged
at the buttons of his shirt and then closed her
eyes in mute pleasure when she had finally revealed the tanned male expanse of his chest.

Lovingly she buried her face against him,
closing her eyes and breathing in his scent before delicately licking at the small indentation
in the middle of his chest, discovering the
faintly salty male taste that was exclusively
his.

'Verity,' Silas groaned.

'I want to,' Verity protested. 'I want to
know every bit of you, Silas. I want to hold
you, touch you, taste you. I want…'

'You don't know what you're saying,' Silas
warned her.

But gravely and seriously and suddenly
completely adult and mature, suddenly totally
sensually a woman, Verity told him quietly,
'Oh, yes, I do. I want you, Silas,' she told him,
lifting one of his hands and placing it first
against her heart and then against her sex, saying, 'Here,' and 'here,' and then finally lifting

his hand to her temple and repeating softly, 'and here.'

'With all my heart I thee love,' Silas whispered back, taking hold of her hand and pressing a kiss into the palm before placing it against his chest. 'With my body I thee worship.'

Watching her eyes, he placed her hand intimately on his own body. Verity drew in a quick sharp breath of feminine appreciation and urgency, the pulse in her wrist thudding every bit as fiercely as the pulse she could feel throbbing through the urgent shaft of male flesh she was touching. Instinctively her fingers closed over him, delicately learning and knowing him, whilst Silas continued in a thickly changed voice, lifting not the hand that was holding his sex with such feminine tenderness and love, but her other to his own forehead. 'With my mind I thee honour, with everything that is me I commit myself to you now, Verity. Nothing ever can and ever will break the bond we are forming between us tonight. Nothing…'

'Nothing…' Verity repeated softly, and beneath her fingertips she could feel the hot, hard shaft of his sex harden even further and begin to pulse in ever fiercer demand.

The first time he entered her Verity cried out, not in pain but in exultation, clinging passionately to him, welcoming him within her with a heart full of love and joy, her emotions so charged and heightened that the feel of him within her, the knowledge of the intimacy, the love they were sharing, the bond they were creating, brought quick, emotional tears to her eyes.

Seeing them, Silas immediately cursed himself under his breath and started to withdraw from her, believing that he had hurt her. Quickly Verity reassured him, explaining in a choked voice that it was the pleasure of having him within her that had caused them, and not the pain.

Later he told her that what they had shared was just the beginning of the pleasure he intended to give her, the special sensual intimacy they would share.

'*You* are my *special* garden, Verity,' he told her as he lovingly caressed her warmly naked body. 'My most private, secret garden where what flowers between us is special and magical and for us alone.'

'And which, one day, hopefully will bear fruit,' Verity continued, picking up on his theme as she blissfully ran her fingertips down his spine, revelling in her right to touch him and to be with him. 'But not for a long time yet,' she added drowsily. 'And I don't suppose that Uncle Toby will want me to have more than the most basic maternity leave…'

'Maternity leave?' Silas checked her, his body suddenly tensing as he started to frown. 'I know you've said that your uncle expects you to work in the business once you've finished university, but surely what's happened between us changes that? I'm not so sexist that I'd want to prevent you from working if that's what you want, but…'

'It isn't a matter of what *I* want, Silas,' Verity told him slowly. 'My uncle *expects* me to work alongside him in the business and then to take over from him. It means *everything* to him…'

'More than *you* or *your* happiness,' Silas challenged her. 'Or are you trying to tell me that it and he mean more to you than me and our children…?'

'No, of course not…but I owe him so much and he…'

'More than you owe our love?' Silas demanded.

They were on the verge of quarrelling and Verity's eyes filled with hot, hurt tears. Couldn't Silas understand how *difficult* things were for her? Of course she wanted to be with him. How could she not do?

'Please, don't let's spoil things by fighting,' she begged him. Although she sensed that he wanted to continue their discussion, instead he gave a small sigh and said, 'No, you're right. This isn't the time…nor the place…'

'Make love to me again, Silas,' she urged him, and it wasn't until many, many months later that she was mature enough to recognise how dangerously she had begun the habit then—a way of avoiding the issue and sidelining it, and Silas, by distracting his attention away from the future through lovemaking. In fact, it wasn't until Silas himself accused her of it that she was forced to recognise just what she was doing and by then...

'I'll love you for ever. You're everything I've ever wanted, everything I *will* ever want,' Silas promised her the following morning as they lay entwined with one another in bed, her body still sleek and damp from the passion of their recent lovemaking.

Only it hadn't been a promise which he had kept. It had been a promise he had broken, just as he had broken her heart and almost broken her.

CHAPTER FOUR

HER first impression that the town hadn't changed had been an erroneous one, Verity acknowledged as she dumped the supermarket carrier bags on the kitchen table.

She had spent the afternoon exploring her old environment before calling in at an out-of-town supermarket to fill her car with petrol and buy some food.

The layout of the town centre might essentially be the same but many of the small shops she remembered from her girlhood had gone, to be replaced with what she privately considered to be an over-representation of building society and estate agents offices. The pedestrianisation of the town centre itself, though, she had to admit, was an improvement, and she had particularly liked the way shady trees had been planted and huge tubs of brightly coloured tumbling summer bedding plants grouped artistically around them. Along with the strategically placed benches, they had created a relaxed, informal, almost continental air to the town centre, which today had been heightened by the fact that the warm summer weather had meant that people had been able to eat outside the square's several restaurants and cafés under the umbrellas decorating the tables and chairs on the pavement. It had been disconcerting, though, to read from a small plaque that the square had been re-designed by Silas as a gift to the town.

If the town centre itself had looked disconcertingly unfamiliar, then so had the faces of the people she had seen around her. She had never made any really close friends during her school-days. The regime imposed by her uncle had prevented that, but there had been girls whose company she could have enjoyed.

Tonight she would ring Charlotte, she promised herself as she started to unpack her provisions. It would be good to hear a friendly voice. She didn't want to think about the consequences of the fact that one of the few adult

voices she had heard since her return had been
that of her ex-lover and that it had been far
from friendly.

A 'friend' had told him about the accident,
he had told her tersely. What exactly did *that*
mean? The term 'friend' applied to a member
of the opposite sex could cover so many pos-
sibilities. Anyway, why should *she* care who
or what this woman was to Silas?

Removing the jacket of the Gucci trouser
suit she was wearing, she opened the fridge
door.

Wearing Gucci to do the supermarket shopping was perhaps a trifle over the top, especially outside Knightsbridge, and even more
especially when the suit in question was white
and had featured extremely prominently in all
the glossies early on in the season, but having
given into Charlotte's pleas and bought the
dratted thing she could hardly leave it hanging
in her wardrobe... Even so... She had fully
registered the several double takes she had received from other shoppers, women clad in the
main in the busy suburban women's uniform

of immaculate neat jeans, white shirt and navy blazer.

She supposed her hair didn't help either, she acknowledged, flipping it back over her shoulder, then taking a clip from her pocket and pinning it up. She had worn it long ever since she could remember. As a teenager she had wanted to have it cut but for once her uncle and Silas had been unanimous in their veto—albeit for very different reasons. Her uncle had always insisted that her hair was neatly tucked into an old-fashioned bun—the kind he remembered his mother wearing—whilst Silas... Silas had whispered to her that first night they had shared together that he had fantasised about taking her hair and wrapping it around his body, feeling its supple silkiness caressing his skin.

She had made that fantasy come true for him, even if she had blushed a little to do so that very first time.

In the years that had passed since then, she had still not had her hair cut—trimmed occasionally, yes, but cut, never—and, until she had sold the company, in obedience to her uncle's wishes she had always worn it rolled into an elegant knot.

She had lost count of the times Charlotte had tried to persuade her to wear it down.

'I'm too old for long, loose hair,' she had protested determinedly.

'Are you crazy?' Charlotte had argued back, adding, 'Have you seen the latest round of jeans ads—the one featuring the back view of a woman with hair down to her waist? She's seventy and she's making one hell of a positive statement about the way women have the right to view ourselves, besides which she looks absolutely stunning. If I had hair like yours— thick, wavy—there's no way you'd ever get me to hide it away.'

'In business, big business, men view long hair on a woman as a sign of weakness. It's probably some kind of Narcissus complex,' Verity had remarked wryly. 'They see long hair and immediately they think, Ah ha…gotcha…she's going to be spending more time in front of the mirror than in front of any sales figures, and then they start rubbing their hands together in glee because they think they're going to put one over on you.'

'Oh, yeah. Let me tell you something, lady,' Charlotte had corrected her after she had finished laughing. 'The reason they're rubbing their hands together in glee is because they're thinking, Wow, that's some woman, *I* want to take her to bed...'

'In other words to them long hair equals bimbo, victim...weakness.'

'Why do I get the distinct impression that somewhere, some time, some man has hurt you very badly?' Charlotte had asked intuitively. But Verity had simply shaken her head. The past, her past, was simply something she was not prepared to talk about—not even to her closest friend.

One thing Verity had noticed, though, when she had been out, and it was something that had caught painfully at her unguarded, vulnerable emotions, had been the number of couples shopping together—and not all of them young. Seeing the loving, tenderly amused looks one couple had exchanged, as the man had reached up to a higher shelf for something the woman had wanted and she had surreptitiously stroked his thigh whilst he did so, had made Verity look away in hot-cheeked sharp awareness of the emotional emptiness of her own life. It didn't have to be that way. Once she had had time to think, to assess and to plan; once she became fully involved in the charities she intended to set up with her uncle's money, then there would be no time for painful regrets about what might have been.

It was seeing Silas that had unsettled her so distressingly, she told herself angrily. Seeing him and listening to him making those outrageous accusations against her.

She stiffened as she heard the doorbell ring. There was no reason for her to think that it might be Silas, of course, but just in case... Forcing her face to assume the expression she normally reserved for the boardroom—the one that said 'Don't even *think* about trying to mess with me'—she headed determinedly for the front door and yanked it open.

'Honor,' she squeaked in startled surprise. 'What on earth are you doing here?'

'I got my pocket money today and I've come to pay the first instalment of the money I owe you for the damage to your car,' Honor told her sturdily, adding before Verity could say anything, 'May I come in? It's so hot…'

'Yes. Of course. Let me get you a cold drink,' Verity offered, leading the way to the kitchen. 'Did you walk here?'

'Mmm…' Honor mumbled as she took a deep gulp of the iced orange juice Verity had poured for her.

'Mmm…real juice!' Honor exclaimed blissfully. 'Wonderful, but it's very expensive,' she told Verity sternly. 'Dad won't buy it—he says I waste it because I never finish it and it's too expensive. He buys it when Myra comes round, though.' She pulled a face. 'Apparently she likes it for breakfast—not that she's ever stayed overnight. She'd like to, though. She thinks I don't know what her game is but I do—a woman always knows,' she concluded wisely. 'She wants to get married again and she wants to marry Dad. He'd be mad if he did—she's poison.' Honor pulled an expressive face. 'She didn't even like the new clothes I made him buy, and I know why—she doesn't want any other woman looking at him.'

Honor had chosen Silas' designer clothes! But Verity didn't have time to digest this information properly before Honor was continuing, 'I've tried to warn him but Dad just can't see it... I suppose he can't see the truth beneath all that make-up she wears. She hates kids as well. That's why she left her first husband. I know... But Dad thinks it's because he wouldn't let her get pregnant...'

Verity gave her a wary look.

'Oh, it's okay, Dad didn't tell me that. He's a great father, the best, but we don't have that kind of relationship. He's pretty much for keeping what he thinks of grown-up things to himself, but I'm not a kid...and I've got my ear to the ground. She's just not good enough for him.'

'How old are you exactly, Honor?' Verity asked her faintly, automatically refilling the now empty glass Honor had extended.

'Ten...' Honor told her promptly.

Ten going on ninety, Verity decided. Did Silas have any inkling of how his daughter felt about her prospective stepmother? she wondered. At least she now knew exactly what the word 'friend' meant when applied to Silas' relationship with his tell-tale girlfriend.

'I'm starving,' Honor told her winningly, 'and Dad's gone out for dinner tonight. I don't suppose...?'

Her aplomb really was extraordinary for someone so young, and perhaps Verity ought to very firmly remind her of the age gap that lay between them and the inadvisability of inviting herself into other people's lives—but she *liked* her, Verity acknowledged, and even if it *was* a weakness within herself she simply couldn't bring herself to dent that luminous youthful pride by pointing out such facts to her.

'I'm afraid I *can't* offer you anything to eat,' she replied gravely instead, intending to tell Honor that she rather thought that her father would disapprove of them having any kind of contact with one another—and not just because *he* obviously considered that she had more or less callously practically run Honor down, thanks to the evidence of his 'girlfriend'. She amended her private thoughts to say gently instead, 'I was planning to eat out.'

'Oh, good.' Honor grinned, telling her frankly, 'I hate cooking too.'

Verity blinked.

'Honor, I *don't* hate cooking,' she protested. 'It's just...'

'There's a terrific Italian place just opened up in town. Italian's my favourite, I love their ice cream puddings,' Honor volunteered.

Totally against her better judgement, Verity knew that she was weakening.

'Mmm...' she agreed. 'I like Italian too...'

Woman to woman they looked at one another.

'You're right,' Verity heard herself saying, a little to her own bemusement. 'Why cook at home when you can eat Italian somewhere else?'

What was she thinking? What was she *doing*? Verity asked herself grimly ten minutes later when she had parked the car in the town centre car park. There would be hell to pay if Silas ever found out, she acknowledged fatalistically, frowning a little as she waited for Honor to get out of the car before activating the central-locking system.

That wasn't by any chance *why* she was doing this, was it? To get at Silas? She was way, way above those kind of childish tit-for-tat manoeuvres, wasn't she? Wasn't she...?

'It's this way,' Honor told her, happily linking her arm through Verity's.

'You should wear your hair down,' she advised Verity seriously as she checked their reflections in a shop window. 'Men like it.'

'Uh-huh...er...do they?'

Heavens, what was wrong with her? *She* shouldn't be the one acting flustered and self-conscious, Verity derided herself.

'The purpose, the point, of being a woman is not to please men or to seek their approval,' she told Honor sternly.

'No, but it sure helps when you want your own way,' Honor told her practically.

Verity gave her an old-fashioned look. 'Your father came to see me,' she told Honor quietly. 'His…friend…Myra…saw the accident and told him about it.'

Honor grimaced. 'Yes, I know. He hasn't grounded me, though, but he was pretty angry about it. He just got angry, though, because he feels guilty that he can't be there all the time for me,' Honor told her with a maturity that caught at Verity's sensitive heart. 'He worries about me—I worry too,' Honor admitted unexpectedly, showing heart-rending vulnerability as she confided reluctantly, 'It isn't much fun—not having a mother. It hurts a lot sometimes.'

'I know,' Verity agreed quietly.

For a moment they looked at one another and then Honor told her quickly, 'Look, the restaurant's here,' directing Verity's attention to the building in front of them. 'Don't let them give us a bad table just because we're

two women eating alone without a man,'
Honor hissed to Verity as they walked inside.

'Two *what*…?' Verity started to question,
but the *maître d'* was already approaching
them and, mindful not only of Honor's stern
admonition but also of the fact that as a potential mentor—not to mention role model—to
the young girl, it behoved her to set a good
example, she looked him firmly in the eye and
said, 'We'd like a table for two, please. That
one over there,' she added, pointing to what
was obviously their 'best' table.

Without batting an eyelid the *maître d'*
swept them both a small bow and agreed,
'Very well, Madam, if you would just follow
me.'

'That was good,' Honor acknowledged glee-
fully when they had been seated.

'No,' Verity corrected her wryly with a grin,
'*that* was Gucci,' she told her flicking her fingertips over her suit. 'It isn't *just* long hair that
men are susceptible to, you know,' she pointed
out drolly, before picking up her menu.

'Ready to order?' she asked Honor several minutes later.

'Mmm...' the young girl agreed.

Raising her hand discreetly, Verity summoned the *maître d'*, waiting until Honor had given him her order before giving her own.

'Oh, and I'd like a glass of the house red as well,' Honor included decidedly.

The *maître d'* was visibly and seriously impressed, as well he might be, Verity acknowledged as, considerably less so, *she* gave Honor a thoughtful look.

'Er...with water,' Honor amended hastily, obviously sensing the veto that was about to leave Verity's lips.

'It's okay,' she told Verity defensively when the waiter had gone. 'Dad lets me—he says it's important for me to grow up learning how to handle alcohol. He says it makes for less mistakes later.'

'Dad said that you used to live here, in town,' Honor commented to Verity once they were eating their starter.

'Er, yes. Yes, I did,' Verity agreed.

'Did you know him then?' Honor asked her.

Verity paused, the forkful of food she had been lifting towards her mouth suddenly un-appetising for all its rich, delicious smell.

'Er…no, I don't think so,' she prevaricated. How much had Silas told his daughter? Not the truth. How could he?

'Did you know my mother?' Honor asked her, startling Verity with the unexpectedness of the question.

'No. No, I didn't,' she told her truthfully. Poor child, and she *was* a child still, for all her quaintly grown-up ways and determined in-dependence, Verity recognised. It couldn't be easy for her, growing up without any real per-sonal knowledge of the woman who had given birth to her.

'She and Dad met when he was staying in London,' Honor told her pragmatically, 'so I didn't think you would. I don't look very much like her.'

'No, you look like your father,' Verity agreed, her heart suddenly jolting against her ribs as the restaurant door opened and the subject of their conversation walked in, accompanied by a woman whom Verity didn't recognise but who she guessed must be his 'friend' Myra.

'What is it?' Honor asked her innocently.

'Your father's just walked in,' Verity told her warningly, but to her surprise, instead of reacting as she had expected, the little girl simply dimpled a wide smile that caused sharp alarm bells to ring in Verity's brain.

'You *knew* he was coming here,' she breathed.

'It's the "in" place to be seen, but Myra won't be very pleased that *we've* got the best table,' Honor told her sunnily.

No, she certainly wasn't, Verity acknowledged, quickly assessing the other woman's angry-mouthed expression, and, what was more, Verity suspected that it wasn't simply the fact that the best table wasn't free that was angering her. *Their* presence—full stop— Verity rather guessed had a very definite something to do with the other woman's ire.

In any other circumstances the sternly con-
demnatory look Silas was sending her would
probably have had her scuttling for the exit,
Verity reflected ruefully, but she could hardly
leave Honor to face her father's wrath alone,
even if perhaps she did semi-deserve it.

Silas was heading for their table, having
bent his head to say something first to his girlfriend, who was now standing glaring vi-
ciously, not so much at her as at Honor, Verity
recognised with a strong surge of protection
towards the young girl.

'Mmm, this is yummy... Hi, Dad,' Honor
acknowledged her father, turning her head to
give him a wide beam.

'Would you like to explain to me what the
hell you think you're doing?' Silas asked
Verity in a dangerously quiet voice, totally ignoring his daughter's sunny greeting.

'Riccardo gave us the best table, Dad,'
Honor chattered on, apparently oblivious to
both Verity's tension and her father's fury.
'Verity said it was because of her suit. It's
Gucci, you know, but I think it was probably

because Riccardo fancied her. He likes straw-
berry blondes,' she added warmly to Verity.
'That's probably why he never gives Myra a
good table,' she told her father, whilst Verity
closed her eyes and sent up a mental prayer,
not just for her own safe deliverance from
Silas' very evident ire, but Honor's as well.
'He doesn't like brunettes... Dad...' She
paused judiciously before refilling her fork
'...do you suppose Myra dyes her hair? *I* think
she must because it's such a very hard shade
of dark brown. What do you think, Verity?'

Verity gulped and shook her head, totally
incapable of making any kind of logical response. She was torn between giving way to
the fit of extremely inappropriate giggles of
feminine appreciation of Honor's masterly un-
dermining of a woman whom Verity could see
quite plainly she considered to be a rival for
her father's attention, and a rather more adult
awareness of the danger of her own situation
and just how little Silas would relish the fact
that *she* was the one to witness his daughter's
artful stratagems.

'What are you doing here, Honor?' Silas turned to his daughter to ask with awful calmness.

'I...I...er...invited her to have dinner with me,' Verity began, immediately rushing to the little girl's defence, but Honor, it transpired, didn't need any defending—rather she seemed positively to enjoy courting her father's fury, looking him straight in the eye.

'I invited Verity to have dinner with me,' she told her father challengingly. 'It was the least I could do after—'

'The least *you* could do?' Shaking his head, he turned from Honor to Verity and told her acidly, 'First you damn near kill my daughter with your dangerous driving and then you, God alone knows by what means, persuade her to have dinner with you. What were you intending to do? Trick her into changing her story just in case I *did* decide to report you to the police? You run her down and then—'

'No, Dad... It wasn't like that...' Honor pushed away her plate and looked quickly from Verity's white face to her father's. 'I...

It wasn't Verity's fault... I...' She swallowed
and then continued bravely, 'It was mine...'

'Yours? But Myra said—'

'It happened exactly how you'd warned me
it would,' Honor ploughed on doggedly. 'I did
just what you told me not to do. I was on my
blades and I didn't think to stop or look and
then I lost control and—'

'Is this true?' Silas asked Verity coldly.

For a moment Verity was tempted to lie and
take the blame, but before she could do so
Honor was speaking again, reaching out to
touch her father's arm.

'Yes. It is true, Dad,' she told him quietly.
'I...I'm sorry... Please don't be mad. I...I
went to see Verity because I want to pay for
the damage to her car out of my spending
money. It was my idea for us to come out for
dinner...'

'Honor. You *know* the rules. What on
earth...? You were *supposed* to be going
straight to Catherine's from school and staying
there tonight.'

'I know that, Dad, but today Catherine said that her aunt and uncle were coming to stay and I knew it was going to be a family sort of thing... I didn't want...' She hung her head before saying gruffly, 'I just wouldn't have felt right being there.'

As she listened to her, Verity's heart went out to her. Underneath her amazingly street-wise exterior she was still, after all, a very vulnerable little girl at heart. A little girl who had never known the love of her mother; a little girl who quite plainly and understandably was jealously protective of her own place in her father's life, to the extent that she quite obviously did not like the woman who she had told Verity was angling to become her father's second wife.

'I think perhaps we should go, Honor,' Verity intervened, gently touching the little girl's arm, summoning the quiet strength of will she had often been forced to use in her boardroom battles. It had never been Verity's style to assume the manner of a 'man'—there *were* other ways of making one's point and any man, anyone, who thought that she could be bullied or pushed around just because she didn't hector or argue very quickly discovered just how wrong they had been.

'I haven't had my pudding,' Honor reminded her stoutly, but Verity could see that she was glad of her protective intervention.

'I've got some fruit and ice cream,' she told her, before turning to Silas and looking him straight in the eye as she said, 'You're quite right, I *should* have checked with you before bringing Honor out—that was *my* mistake. Yours...' She paused and reminded herself that with Honor as an interested audience, never mind the *maître d'* and the now very obviously fuming Myra, this was not the time nor the place to point out where *he* had gone wrong or what his misjudgement had been.

'I'm quite prepared to drive Honor round to her friend's, but I wonder if she might be permitted to finish her supper with me?'

'Oh, yes, Dad. And then you could pick me up from Verity's on the way home,' Honor interrupted her eagerly. 'I'd much rather do that than go to Catherine's.'

'If your pudding is ordered, then I'll ask the *maître d'* to bring another chair and you can stay with Myra and me. I take it *you've* finished your meal,' Silas demanded of Verity coldly.

'No. She hasn't… She hasn't had *her* pudding,' Honor told him indignantly, adding, 'Besides, I don't *want* to be with you and Myra, you know she doesn't like me…'

'Honor,' Silas began warningly, twin bands of anger beginning to burn high on his cheekbones, although, as Verity could see, she herself was more alarmed by his fury than Honor.

'Look, *what's* going on? When are we going to eat?'

All three of them looked up as Myra finally grew tired of waiting on the sidelines and came to join battle.

'I'm sorry,' Silas apologised, giving her a warm smile. But Myra wasn't looking at him. Instead, her eyes were flashing warning signs in Verity's direction, narrowing angrily as she studied Verity's suit.

'I was just explaining to Honor that she could finish her meal with us,' Silas told Myra.

'What? But you're coming back with me so that I can show you that video I've got of my cousin's wedding…' Myra protested, darting a fulminating look at Honor.

'If I stay with you, can I have cappuccino to finish with?' Honor asked Silas.

'Er…' Silas was looking uncertainly from his daughter's face to his girlfriend's. In any other circumstances and with any other man, Verity knew she would have felt quite sympathetic towards him. As it was, tucking down the corners of her mouth so that no one could see the smile curling there, she caught Honor's attention.

'Remember the Bible story of Solomon?' she asked the little girl *sotto voce*.

'Solomon?' Honor whispered back whilst Silas and Myra removed themselves slightly from the table to engage in what looked like a very heated conversation. 'Oh, you mean the one where the two women both claimed the baby and Solomon threatened to cut it in two and let them have half each?' Honor asked her.

'That's the one,' Verity agreed dulcetly. Honor frowned and then suddenly burst out laughing as she saw Verity glance over towards Silas.

'Oh, but Dad isn't a baby,' she protested.

'No, but he *is* your father and sometimes loving someone means letting them make their own decisions,' Verity told her gently.

'But she's not right for him,' Honor protested, and then shrugged her shoulders. 'Okay.'

'Dad...'

'Honor...'

Verity waited as they both started to speak and then both stopped.

'If you're sure you don't mind giving Honor supper and keeping her with you until I can collect her,' Silas told Verity distantly.

'*I* don't mind at all,' Verity responded truthfully, adding as she smiled at Honor, 'In fact, it will be a pleasure.'

'Goodie… There goes Myra's plan for showing my father the tempting prospect of getting married via her cousin's wedding video,' Honor exulted several minutes later as she and Verity exited the restaurant, Honor clutching a huge double portion of rich ice cream that the now-besotted *maître d'* had insisted on giving her complete with a bowl of ice to keep it chilled until they got home.

'I shouldn't be too sure about that,' Verity warned her. 'Myra looks one very determined lady to me…'

'Determined she might be, but Dad is catastrophically old-fashioned about me going to bed early on school nights. There's no way he's going to be able to go home with Myra tonight.'

Verity stopped walking and swung round to glance incredulously at Honor.

'Did you deliberately plan all of this?' she asked her bluntly.

Honor's face assumed a hurt expression.

'Me… I'm ten years old,' she reminded Verity.

'Yeah...but somehow you seem so much older,' Verity responded feelingly.

As they walked in amicable female companionship towards Verity's parked car, Honor allowed herself to relax.

Part one of her plan was working. What would Verity say, she wondered, if she told her that she had recognised her straight away on the day of the accident from a photograph of her she had found in her father's desk? Her father needed rescuing from Myra and it was high time, Honor had already decided, that she had a mother—one of her own choosing!

She looked sideways at Verity—why had she fibbed about not knowing her father? She was tempted to ask but she decided it might be best not to rush things so much...not yet. Honestly, grown-ups, they were so slow... But it was just as she and her friend Catherine had said earlier this afternoon when she had jubilantly told her all about Verity. Sometimes grown-ups didn't know where their own best interests lay, so it was just as well that she, Honor, was here to show them.

What she needed to do now was to keep her father and Myra apart, but if her plans worked out as she knew they would that shouldn't prove too difficult—Catherine had her instructions!

Verity gave her a surprised look as Honor suddenly slipped a small, slightly grubby hand into her own and beamed a huge smile up at her.

'It's no good trying to get round me like that,' Verity warned her severely, adding untruthfully, 'and, besides, I can't make cappuccino…'

'No, but I bet Myra can,' Honor told her. 'She was *really* frothing at the mouth, wasn't she?' she observed dispassionately.

'Honor…' Verity warned, and then spoiled it by suddenly giving way to an uncontrollable fit of the giggles.

'Verity…just a moment, please…

Verity's body tensed in shock as she heard Silas calling out curtly from behind her. She had already unlocked the car for Honor to get inside it and now, as she too saw her father, Honor opened the door.

Silas shook his head and told her crisply, 'You stay where you are, please, Honor. I want to have a few words with Verity...in private!'

Verity wasn't sure which of them looked the more wary—herself or Honor. What she *was* sure of, though, was that she could feel her skin turning a very definite shade of mollified pink as Honor, after one look at her father's stern 'I mean business' expression, quietly closed the passenger door of Verity's car.

Equally reprehensibly feebly, Verity discovered that she herself was moving several yards away from her car, mirroring the way that Silas was moving out of Honor's potential earshot. Just to make sure that Silas knew and understood that, unlike his daughter, *she* was not someone he could talk down to or tell what to do, before he could tell her whatever it was that had brought him hotfoot out of the restaurant and away from Myra's side, Verity demanded coldly, 'Please be quick, Silas, I still haven't eaten my pudding.'

'Ice cream?' His mouth took on a mocking twist. 'As *I* remember it you were always more of a cheese and biscuits woman and—'

Immediately Verity's eyes flashed. How dared he remind her of the intimacy they had once shared; of everything they had once been to one another, now when he...?

'Is *that* why you came running after us—to remind me because *I* opted for ice cream over cheese and biscuits? *My* tastes have changed, Silas...just like yours...'

But sharp though her words were, for some unaccountable reason, as she said them, Verity discovered that she was looking at his mouth and remembering...

A shudder of self-contempt shook her as she acknowledged just *what* she was remembering, her eyes darkening as she did so.

Did Silas remember that ice cream they had shared so long ago, and, if he did, did he remember too the way he had teased her by offering her the last mouthful of it and then, when she had taken it, kissing her through the icy-cold taste, his lips, his mouth, his tongue,

so velvet-hot and sensuous against her lips,
and then when the ice cream had melted his
kiss becoming so passionate that *it* had practically melted *her*?

Her face on fire, Verity made to take a step
back from him, but to her consternation Silas
immediately reached out to stop her, his hand
grasping her upper arm in a grip she knew it
would be impossible for her to break.

'Verity,' he began, his voice unexpectedly
thick and husky as though...

Quickly Verity cast a lash-veiled look at
him. Surely his own colour was slightly higher
than it should have been?

Because he was angry? It certainly couldn't
be because he was aroused, could it?

Unexpectedly he gave his head a small
shake, as though trying to dispel some un-
wanted thought, and when he spoke again his
voice was much crisper.

'Honor is ten years old...a child... I don't
want her getting hurt...' he began warningly.

Immediately Verity took umbrage. How
dared he suggest that *she* might hurt Honor?

'If you're implying that I might hurt her,' she told him furiously, 'then you're wrong. In fact, if you believe that Honor *is* being hurt I should look far closer to home for the source if I were you.'

There was a moment's shocked pause before he demanded in disbelief, 'Are you trying to say that *I* might hurt her...?'

Taking advantage of his momentary lapse in concentration, Verity pulled herself free of his grip and started to turn towards the car.

'Verity, I haven't finished—' she heard him saying furiously to her, but Verity had had enough—more than enough if the way her body, her senses, were still responding to the memory of that shared ice cream so long ago was anything to go by.

'Oh, but I think you have,' she corrected him through gritted teeth and then stopped abruptly, shocked to discover that for some reason all his attention seemed to be focused on her mouth. Instinctively she raised protective fingers to her lips, her whole body starting to tremble.

'Verity…' she heard him saying roughly, but she shook her head, unable to listen to whatever it was he wanted to say, whatever further contemptuous criticism he wanted to hurl at her unprotected heart.

'Go away, Silas,' she demanded shakily. 'Go back to Myra…'

And without waiting to see his reaction she hurried quickly towards her car and opened the door.

'What did Dad want?' Honor asked uncertainly several minutes later, once Verity had negotiated their way out of the car park.

'Er…he wanted to tell me that you weren't to have too much ice cream,' Verity fibbed, making up the first excuse she could think of.

'Not much chance of that. By the time we get back it will all be melted…gone…' Honor told her in disgust.

Gone…like their love… Verity bit down hard on her bottom lip. Ice cream and Silas' kisses. Funny how sharply painful the sweetest things could sometimes become!

CHAPTER FIVE

'IT'S gone ten o'clock,' Verity told Honor worriedly. 'I thought your father would have been here by now—you said he wouldn't want you to be out late.'

'Mmm... I know.'

Honor seemed far less perturbed about her father's absence than she was, Verity noticed, which surprised her. She would have thought that, given Honor's obvious dislike of Myra, she would have become at least a little anxious about the fact that Silas was quite obviously lingering with the woman rather longer than Honor had originally intimated.

Perhaps Myra had prevailed on him to take her home after all, and, once there, no doubt she had insisted that he remain for a nightcap and of course, whilst he was drinking it, she had no doubt put on the video. 'Just so that he could see a few minutes of it.' And then, of course, it would be a small step—a *very* small step for her kind of woman—from that to turning down the lights and refilling Silas' glass, insisting that there was no need for him to rush and that surely Honor could miss a morning of school for once...

Verity could virtually hear the enticing personal arguments she would purr into his ear as she slipped onto the sofa beside him and placed her hand on his jacket, supposedly to remove a bit of non-existent fluff, before sliding it up onto his shoulder and then caressing the back of his neck where his hair curled thick and dark. Verity closed her eyes. She could remember so clearly just how that felt—how *she* had felt, how just the intimacy simply of touching him like that had made her go weak at the knees, all melting, yielding, wanting womanhood.

'Verity, are you all right?'

'What...? Er...' guiltily Verity opened her eyes '...er, yes...' she fibbed, hot-cheeked, hurriedly getting up so that she could avoid meeting the innocence of Honor's eyes.

'Perhaps we should ring the restaurant,' she began hurriedly. 'I—'

'No... No... I don't think that would be a good idea,' Honor instantly denied. 'I mean, Dad was so angry, wasn't he? And...' But despite what she had said Verity couldn't help noticing that Honor herself did keep looking at the silent telephone.

'Perhaps he's been delayed...a flat tyre or something like that,' she offered comfortingly.

'How long is your hair?' Honor asked, moving their conversation away from her father's late arrival.

'Er...'

'Take it down now,' Honor urged her, reaching out to tweak some of the constraining pins from Verity's hair before she could stop her.

Suspecting that the little girl was more disturbed by her father's non-appearance than she wanted to admit, Verity gave in.

'Oh, it's lovely,' Honor told her in open and honest admiration when all the pins were finally removed and Verity had quickly pulled the small brush she kept in her handbag through her soft curls.

'It's getting too long. I should really have it cut,' Verity said ruefully.

'Oh, no, you mustn't,' Honor told her, gently stroking her fingers through it.

Verity felt her heart jerk and then almost stop. Once, a long time ago, a *lifetime* ago it seemed now, Silas had touched her hair just like that and spoken similar words to her.

'No, don't ever have it cut,' he had whispered to her. 'I love it so much—I love *you* so much.'

Instinctively she closed her eyes.

'What's the matter? You look awfully sad,' Honor told her.

There was a huge lump in Verity's throat.

'I—' she began, and then stopped as the phone suddenly rang. Honor reached it first but, a little to Verity's surprise, she waited for her to pick up the receiver.

'Verity?'

There was no mistaking the crisp tones of Silas' voice.

'Yes. Yes, Silas…'

'Look, I can't talk now. There's been an emergency. I'm at the garden centre. The police called me out. Someone reported seeing intruders trying to break in. So far we haven't found any signs of anyone but it looks as though I could be tied up here for some time. Honor…'

'Honor's fine with me, unless you want me to take her to her friend's,' Verity assured him as calmly as she could. Why was her heart beating so frantically fast, her pulse racing, her mouth dry, her whole body reacting to the sound of his voice as if…as though…?

'No. It's probably best if she stays with you. I don't know what time I'm going to be through here…'

'Don't worry,' Verity assured him. 'She'll be fine here with me. Would you like to speak with her?'

Without waiting for his response, she handed the receiver over to Honor, before walking over to the window and putting her hands to her suddenly hot face.

What on *earth* was the matter with her? She was reacting like…like a woman in love… A deep shudder ran through her. Impossible. No. No way. Not again. Not a second time.

'Not a second time what?' Honor asked her curiously.

Wide-eyed, Verity turned round and looked at her. She hadn't heard Honor replace the telephone receiver, never mind realised that she had spoken out loud.

'Er…nothing… Look, it could be some time before your father gets here. If you want to go to bed…'

'No. Well, yes, perhaps that might be a good idea,' Honor allowed. 'I haven't got anything to wear, though,' she reminded Verity.

'That's okay, you can sleep in your undies for tonight,' Verity told her practically.

'I don't very much like the dark,' Honor said as they walked upstairs. 'Will you…will you stay with me until I go to sleep?'

Once again Verity was reminded of the fact that Honor was only a very young girl—a motherless young girl—and Verity herself knew what that meant and all about the private desperate tears cried into one's pillow at night. Tears for the love and want of a mother's arms—a mother's care. Honor had her pride, Verity could see, but she could see as well that she also had her vulnerability, her need to be reassured, her need to be mothered.

'Yes, of course I will,' Verity agreed warmly, giving her hand a small squeeze.

'I'm not very keen on the dark myself,' she added.

In the end it was another hour before Honor was finally in bed—Verity's bed, since it was the only one that was made up and since Honor had announced that she liked Verity's room best of all. 'Because it smells of you,' she had so engagingly told Verity.

Who could resist that kind of persuasion? And, for the second time, Verity had been all too intimately reminded of hearing Honor's father make just such a similar comment, although in a vastly different context—a context far too intimate and personal to *even* allow herself to think about in the presence of anyone else, never mind Silas' young daughter.

'Why not? Why don't you want me to?' he had asked her thickly when she had tried to push him away the first time he had bent his head towards the most intimate part of her body.

'Because…because…' Awkwardly she had struggled to explain how both shocked and excited she had felt at the thought of being caressed so, so personally by him, of having his lips, his mouth, kiss the most delicate and sensitive part of her body.

'It just doesn't seem right,' she had told him shakily in the end. 'I mean, it's…' Pleadingly she had lifted her gaze to his. 'Silas, I don't… it's…'

'It's just another way of showing you how much I love you,' Silas had told her gently. 'If you don't want me to then I won't, but I want to enjoy the scent and taste of you—the real you—so much, Verity. I know what you're thinking…how you're feeling…but I promise you that it will be all right.'

'It seems so… It makes me feel so…so nervous and afraid and so…excited at the same time,' she had confessed. 'All sort of squirmy and…and…'

'It makes me feel the same,' Silas had told her in a deep voice. 'Only even more so. Will you let me, Verity? I promise I'll stop if you want me to. It's just…' He had paused and looked deep into her eyes, making her heart thump against her chest wall in great shuddering thuds.

'I want to make you mine in every way there is. To know you so completely; to love you so completely.'

And when eventually he had lain her tenderly on the bed and bent his head over her body, when she had felt his tongue tip gently rimming the very centre of her sexual being, Verity hadn't wanted him to stop at all, not at all, not ever, as she had cried out frantically to him when the racking paroxysms of pleasure had seized hold of her, caught her up and dislodged from her mind any thought she might ever have had about not wanting the pleasure that Silas had been giving her, the intimacy...

'Verity...'

With a start Verity dragged her mind and her thoughts back to the present.

'It's a very big bed, isn't it?' Honor told her in a small voice. 'Do you always sleep in a big bed like this?'

'M...mostly,' Verity confirmed.

'It must feel very lonely. Haven't you ever wanted to get married, have children?' Honor asked her.

'It's after eleven o'clock,' Verity warned her, sidestepping the question, knowing that the only honest answer she could give her was no answer to give the ten-year-old daughter of the man whose wife she had hoped to be.

'Stay with me,' Honor whispered again, a small hand creeping out from beneath the bed-clothes to hold onto Verity's.

Watching her ten minutes later as she lay next to her, Verity felt a tug of love on her heartstrings so strong that Honor's small hand might actually have been physically wrapped around them.

'Stop it,' she warned herself sternly. 'Don't you dare start daydreaming along those lines… Don't you dare!'

Very gingerly Verity eased her arm from beneath Honor's sleeping body. It ached slightly and had started to go a little numb. Disconcertingly, though, she discovered as she slid carefully off the bed, she actually missed the warm young weight of Honor's body.

The knowledge that she would probably never marry and have children of her own had been something she had pushed to the back of her mind in recent years. A child or children that she would have to bring up on her own had never been an option for her—her own childhood had given her extremely strong views about a child's need to feel secure and, to Verity, the kind of security *she* had craved so desperately as a child had come all neatly wrapped up with two parents.

In the early years after her breakup with Silas she'd had virtually only to see a young couple out with a small child to feel pierced with misery and envy.

Another woman, a different woman, might, on learning that the man she had loved, the man who had promised always to love her, had married someone else, have hardened her heart against her own emotions and made herself find someone else, built a new life for herself with a new man in it, but Verity had never been able to do that. For one thing the business had meant that she simply hadn't had the time to form new relationships and for another... For another, for a long time she had felt so hurt and betrayed, so convinced that Silas was the only man she could ever love, that she simply hadn't tried.

But there had still been that sense of loss, that small, sharp ache of envy for other young women who'd had what she hadn't: a man to love and their child.

But now she felt she was far too mature to give in to such feelings.

'What rubbish,' Charlotte had told her forthrightly recently when she had brought up the matter and Verity had said as much to her.

'For one thing you are not even in your late thirties, and for another, women in their early forties are giving birth to their first child nowadays. Neither can you start telling me that you can't spare the time and that the business is too demanding—you don't *have* the business any more.'

'I don't have a partner either,' Verity had felt bound to point out.

'That could easily be remedied,' Charlotte had told her firmly, 'and you know it!'

'Perhaps I'm simply not the maternal type.' Verity had shrugged, anxious to change the subject.

'Come off it,' Charlotte had scoffed. 'You know my two adore you.'

And she loved them, Verity acknowledged now as she tiptoed towards the bedroom door, but something about Honor had touched her heart and her emotions had really shaken her.

Because she was Silas' child?

If anything, surely that should make her resent and dislike her and not...? It was certainly plain that Myra did not feel in the least bit maternal towards her intended future step-daughter. Was it Honor herself she didn't like, or did she perhaps simply resent the fact that she was the physical evidence that Silas had loved another woman? Myra certainly hadn't struck her as the emotionally insecure type.

As Verity opened the bedroom door, Honor moved in her sleep and muttered something. Holding her breath, Verity waited until she was sure she had settled down again and, leaving the bedroom door open and the landing light on, she went quickly downstairs.

It was gone twelve. How much longer would Silas be?

Her discarded suit jacket was lying on the chair where she had left it. Automatically she picked it up and folded it neatly, smoothing the soft fabric. Her uncle would have thoroughly disapproved of her buying something so impractical in white and in a delicately luxurious fabric. Clothes to him had simply been a necessary practicality. Verity could still remember how surprised and thrilled she had been when she and Silas had been walking through town one day and he had stopped her outside a boutique window and, indicating the dress inside, told her tenderly, 'That would suit you...'

The dress in question had been a silky halter-necked affair, backless, the fabric scattered with pretty feminine flowers, and it had also been a world away from the type of clothes she had normally worn: sturdy jeans, neatly pleated skirts, dully sensible clothes bought under the stern eye of her uncle's sixty-year-old Scottish housekeeper.

'Oh, Silas, it's lovely,' she had breathed, 'but it's far too...too pretty for me...'

'*Nothing* could ever be *too* pretty for you,' Silas had returned softly, adding huskily, 'Not pretty enough, maybe...'

'Oh, Silas...' she had whispered, blushing.

'Oh, Verity,' he had teased her back but, later in the week, when he had arrived with a present for her that had turned out to be the

dress, the look in his eyes when he had persuaded her to model it for him had made her
blush for a very, very different reason.

She had protested, of course, that he
shouldn't have bought her something so personal nor so expensive.

'Why not?' he had countered. 'You're the
woman I love, the woman I'm going to marry.'

She had been so young and naive then, assuming that he'd accepted that even as Silas'
wife she'd owe it to her uncle to do as he
wished and take her place in his business. She
had known too, of course, that Silas hadn't
been happy about the silent but ostrich-like
way she had convinced herself that it would
all work out and had pushed it to the back of
her mind. Silas would surely come to respect
her point of view. They were young and in
love—how could anything so mundane as duty
come between them? She had been too dazed
with love and happiness to guess that Silas
might still see her role as his future wife in a
far different light from that in which she did
herself.

Through the sitting-room window Verity saw the headlights of a car coming up the drive. Silas! It had to be.

She opened the front door to him, putting her finger to her lips as she warned him, 'Honor's asleep.'

He looked tired, she recognised, deep lines etched either side of his mouth and tension very evident in the way he moved as he followed her into the house. For some inexplicable reason these indications of the fact that he was no longer a carefree young man in his twenties increased rather than detracted from his masculinity, Verity realised, her heartbeat quickening as the adrenalin kicked into her system and sent a surge of dangerous emotion racing through her veins.

'Was everything all right at the garden centre?' she asked him shakily as he followed her into the kitchen.

Best not to look at him. Not yet. Not until she had herself fully and properly under control. Not that that shuddery, all-too-familiar sensation within her body *meant* anything, of course, it was just…just… Well, she certainly didn't want him looking at her face and recognising anything that might possibly be familiar to him.

'Well, there were no signs of anyone having broken in,' Silas told her tiredly. 'I checked and then double-checked the place and the alarm and everything seemed okay, but the police say that they had a definite tip-off that the place was being broken into and it always leaves you worrying. You know the sort of thing—create a false alarm and then when all the fuss has died down… We've got a hell of a lot of valuable young plants there at the moment, plus a delivery of antique garden statues which I've acquired for one of my clients. It's insured but…' He changed the subject. 'Thanks for looking after Honor for me.' He stopped and grimaced as his obviously empty stomach gave a protesting growl.

'You're hungry.' Verity looked at him. 'Would you like something to eat…?'

He started to shake his head and then stopped as his stomach gave another, louder, protest.

'It isn't anything much,' Verity warned him without waiting for him to make any refusal. 'Just some pâté and French bread…'

Behind her as she busied herself at the fridge, Verity could hear him groan.

'That sounds marvellous,' he told her, admitting, 'I'm famished and I missed out on lunch altogether today.'

'But you *had* dinner,' Verity began as she removed the pâté and some salad, 'and you always used to enjoy Italian.'

'So did you… Remember when I flew out to New York to see you and you took me all around the Italian restaurants you'd discovered…?'

Verity looked at him.

'Yes,' she agreed huskily. 'Yes, I do.'

It had been a brief, a far too brief, visit—a cheap flight he had managed to get, involving only a two-night stay, his visit a surprise to her on her birthday.

She had cried with joy when he'd arrived and she had cried again—*wept* with misery when he had left, but those tears had been

nothing to the ones she had cried the day she
had read of his marriage to someone else.

'Unfortunately Myra isn't as keen on Italian
food as I am and after... Well, we left the restaurant shortly after you—the call came
through from the police on my mobile before
we could order.'

'It isn't much,' Verity told him again as she
put the plate of pâté and salad she had just
prepared onto the table in front of him and then
went to cut the bread.

'Not much! It's *wonderful*, manna from
heaven,' Silas told her fervently.

'Cappuccino?' Verity asked him quizzically
as she handed him the bread basket.

It had always been a bit of a joke between
them that he had loved the rich chocolate-
sprinkled coffee so much. She didn't need to
guess where Honor had got *her* sweet tooth
from.

'Mmm...this pâté's good. Did you buy it
locally?' Silas asked her.

Shaking her head, Verity turned away from
him. Despite what Honor had assumed, she
was, in fact, a very good self-taught cook.

'Actually, I made it myself,' she told him truthfully, and she could see what he was thinking from the way he looked from his plate to her expensive and impractical white trousers.

'Not wearing this,' she told him slightly tartly.

He had almost finished eating and had started to frown again. 'I'd better go up and get Honor,' he told her. 'I'm sorry you got landed with her this evening... It's one of the trials of being a single parent that...'

'Yes. It must have been hard for you, losing your wife,' Verity forced herself to acknowledge.

'Nowhere near as hard as it was for her to lose her life, nor Honor to lose her mother,' he countered harshly, before adding equally grimly, as he glanced at her unbanded wedding finger. 'Obviously, you've never married.'

'No,' Verity agreed coolly. 'The business—' she began, but Silas wouldn't allow her to finish.

He interrupted her with a harsh, 'Don't tell me. *I* know…remember?'

He started to get up as Verity reached to remove his plate, her hair accidentally falling forward and brushing his face as they both moved at the same time.

Immediately Verity tensed, lifting her hand to push her hair off her face, but Silas, on his feet by this time, got there first. The sensation of his fingers in her hair was so familiar, so intimate, that she instinctively closed her eyes.

'Verity…' she heard Silas groan, and then the next minute she was in his arms and he was kissing her with a fierce, hungry, angry, passion that brought her defences crashing down so that immediately and helplessly she was responding to him, the years rolling back so that she was a girl again, so that they were a couple, a *pair* again, so that there was no-where that it was more natural for her to be than here in his arms, *nothing* that was more natural for her to *feel* than what she was feel-ing right now, nothing it was more natural for her to *want* than what she was wanting right now.

Beneath his mouth and hands her body threw off the shackles she had so sternly imposed on it—he was hers again and she was his. Hers to reach out and touch, as she was doing right now, slipping her fingertips into the gap she had miraculously found between the buttons on his shirt, feeling the solid, familiar heat of his skin. Without realising what she was doing, she unfastened one of the shirt buttons that was preventing her from touching him as she wanted to do.

Beneath his mouth she made a small, contented sound of triumph and pleasure at being able to spread her hands fully over his chest with nothing in the way to bar her sensual exploration of his naked skin.

He felt so good, so Silas, so wonderfully familiar. He even tasted just as she had remembered. Automatically Verity pressed closer to him, shuddering deliciously as she felt his hands slide down her back to cup her bottom, lifting her even deeper into his body.

She could feel the urgency, the hunger, the need, in the way he touched her, running his hands over all her body as he continued to kiss her with increasing passion.

The kitchen was full of the sound of their heightened breathing, the electric crackle of hands against cloth, the silky whisper of skin against skin.

'It's been so long,' Verity whispered emotionally between their kisses. 'I've wanted...'

I've wanted you so much, she was just about to say, but suddenly she stiffened. From upstairs Verity heard the bathroom door open. Silas must have heard it too because he immediately released her, saying tautly, 'This shouldn't be happening. Blame it on the frustration of the evening...'

The frustration? Verity's hands were shaking so much she had to hold them out of sight behind her back as she came back down to earth with a sickening jolt.

What was Silas *saying* to her? That it was *his* sexual frustration at having to leave Myra which had caused him to kiss her?

For a moment she thought she was actually going to be sick. A pain, like red-hot twisting knives, was shredding her emotions. Silas hadn't been thinking about *her* at all. All that passion, all that need, all that *wanting* she had felt in him, had *not* been for her at all and she, like a complete idiot, had virtually been on the point of telling him, revealing to him…

Turning away from him so that he couldn't see her face, she told him quietly, 'Honor's obviously awake.'

'I'll go up and get her,' Silas announced curtly. 'Thanks for looking after her for me.'

'I didn't do it for *you*,' Verity told him fiercely. 'I did it for *her*.'

She still couldn't risk turning round. She daredn't, just in case… Just in case what? Just in case Silas guessed what she had been thinking…feeling…wanting…? His pity was something she couldn't bear. His scorn and his rejection would be hard enough to stomach—almost as hard as the knowledge that for the second time he was rejecting her in favour of another woman, letting her *know* that he simply didn't want her—but if she should look at him now and see pity in his eyes...

Quickly she headed for the kitchen door.

'I'll show you which room Honor's in,' she told him without looking at him.

Honor was back in bed when Verity pushed open the bedroom door. When she saw her father she smiled winningly at him.

'Can I stay here with Verity tonight?' she asked.

'No, you can't,' Silas denied sharply, softening his denial by explaining, 'I'm sure Verity's far too busy...'

'You're not, are you, Verity?' Honor appealed.

Verity hesitated. What could she say?

'Perhaps another time,' she offered as Silas gathered up Honor's clothes and stood waiting determinedly with them.

The house felt empty once they had gone.

Oh, but how could she have been so stupid as to overreact like that just because...? No wonder Silas had felt it necessary to make it

clear to her that there had been nothing personal in that kiss he had given her. She could
feel her face starting to burn with humiliation
and pain. As she began to tidy up the kitchen,
a small item on the floor caught her eye.
Frowning, she bent to pick it up. It was a button—a man's shirt button. Her face burned
even more hotly. She must have *ripped* it off
when she had... Quickly she swallowed. She
had never been driven by her sexuality and
even when she and Silas had been lovers she
had always been the more passive partner. She
could certainly never remember having virtually ripped the shirt off his back before.
Angrily she put her hands to her hot face. The
last thing she needed was for Silas to start
thinking that she was holding some kind of
torch for him...that she still *wanted* him, that
she was stupid enough to still be hurting over
the way he had treated her.

From now on, when they met—*if* they
met—she was going to have to make it very
clear to him that tonight's kiss was something
as little wanted or relished by her as it had
been by him!

CHAPTER SIX

'DAD.'

'Mmm…' Silas glanced down at his daughter's head as she sat next to him in the car.

'When Verity lived here before, were you friends?'

'What makes you ask that?' Silas questioned her sharply.

'Nothing.' Honor smiled, looking up at him. 'Well, were you?'

'No.' Silas told her curtly.

'Yes. That's what she said.'

Silas frowned.

'She's very pretty, though, isn't she?' Honor continued sunnily. 'Riccardo certainly thought so.'

'Very,' Silas agreed through gritted teeth. As a young girl Verity has possessed a natural, wholesome, sweet prettiness, but as a woman she had matured into someone whose subtle sensuality...

His favourite plants were always those that took a little bit of knowing; whose attractions were not necessarily flashingly visible at first glance. He had never liked anything overblown nor obvious and Verity... Just now, kissing her, he had been overwhelmed by the urge, by the memory of a certain night they had spent together in the heat of her small New York flat when, during their lovemaking, she had wrapped her legs around him and...

Tonight, watching the way she had moved in that silky white suit she had been wearing, remembering just how lovely and equally silky and feminine her legs were...

'I really like her and she's going to be *my* friend,' Honor informed him. 'Can I invite her round for tea tomorrow?'

'What? No, you can't. You've got school in the morning and homework.'

'No, I haven't. We're having a leave day— I told you last week.'

'What?' Silas looked at her and groaned.

'Honor, why on earth didn't you remind me of that earlier?' he demanded. 'I've got a site meeting in the morning that I can't put off.'

'You should have left me at Verity's,' Honor told him practically. 'You'll have to ring her and ask her if she can look after me tomorrow.'

'What? No way. What about Catherine?'

'No.' Honor shook her head firmly. 'She's got her aunt and uncle staying, remember?'

Silas groaned again.

When Honor had been a baby he had employed a succession of full-time live-in nannies to take care of her when he wasn't there, also taking her into work with him when he could, but the situation was more complicated now that Honor was growing up. For one thing she was extremely independent and diabolically good at getting her own way so that finding the right kind of person—someone firm enough for her to respect and yet young enough not to be too restrictive with her—was proving increasingly difficult. Anna helped out when he could spare her from the garden centre, but they were too busy just now for her to be away from the centre all day.

His last housekeeper had left after Silas had made it plain that she was employed to take care of Honor's needs and not his own, and since then he had been relying increasingly on a patchwork of haphazard arrangements, getting by on a wing and a prayer and the good offices of kind friends.

If he hadn't hit such a busy patch with the business, he would have had time to advertise and sort something more permanent out, but as it was…

'I expect Myra was really cross when you had to leave to go to the garden centre,' Honor commented.

Silas gave her a wry look.

'Just a little,' he agreed.

The truth was that Myra had been furious. She was not a particularly maternal woman. In fact, her own two sons from her marriage lived with their father and his new partner. Silas knew perfectly well that becoming his wife was Myra's goal but being Honor's doting stepmother was the last thing the woman wanted.

She was a woman who, as she had told him quite openly, had a very high sex drive—so far, despite all the encouragement she had given him, Silas had kept their relationship on a purely platonic footing. Perhaps he was out of step with modern times, but sex for sex's sake was something that didn't appeal to him. It never had, which was why...

Silas looked down again at his daughter's dark head. As always when he thought of Honor's mother he was filled with a mixture of guilt and regret.

Neither of them had ever imagined when Sarah had conceived Honor that giving birth to her would result in Sarah losing her own life. If they had...

It had been Sarah herself who had suggested that they should have the pregnancy terminated—neither of them, after all, had been thinking of a baby when Honor had been conceived—but Silas had persuaded her not to go ahead with it.

'I can't afford to bring up a baby,' she had told him frantically.

'I can,' Silas had replied.

A week later they had been married and just over seven months after that Honor had been born.

Forty-eight hours after giving birth Sarah had been dead despite everything that the doctors had done to try and save her. Nothing had been able to stop the massive haemorrhaging which had ended her life and, in the end, the doctors had told Silas that there was simply nothing they could do, that no amount of blood transfusions were going to help, that her body was too far in shock for them to be able to risk any kind of emergency surgery.

She had died without ever seeing Honor.

It hadn't been easy in those early years being totally responsible for a motherless girl child. His own parents had been retired and living abroad, and he had been determined that since he was Honor's only parent he was going to be as involved in her life and as much 'there' for her as he possibly could be, and so he had learned to change nappies without flinching, to bring up wind and to correctly interpret what all those different baby cries meant. But then, almost as soon as he had mastered those complexities, Honor had found new ways to tax his parenting skills—was still finding new ways to tax them, he admitted ten minutes later as he ushered her upstairs to her own bedroom, newly decorated last year for her birthday since she had announced that the 'Barbie' colour scheme and decor she had insisted on having for her sixth birthday was now totally passé and far too babyish for a girl of her new maturity.

In its place her room was now resplendent with everything necessary for a devout and ardent fan of the latest popular 'girl band'.

'I really like Verity,' Honor told him drowsily as he was tucking her up. 'I wish…'

'Go to sleep,' Silas said.

He had reached the doorway and was just about to switch off the light when she called out, 'Da-ad.'

'Yes.' Silas waited.

Honor sat bolt upright in her bed and eyed him seriously. 'You do know, don't you, that I'm getting to an age where I need to have a woman to talk to?'

Silas wasn't deceived. Honor, as he well knew, could run rings around a woman four times her age—could and, exasperatingly, very often did.

'You know what I mean,' Honor stressed. 'There are things I need to know…girl-type things…'

Silas gave her a sceptical look. He and Honor had always had a very open and honest relationship, no subject was taboo between them, and he had assumed that when the time came the subject of Honor's burgeoning womanhood and sexuality would be one they would cope with together. Honor, or so she was implying, had other ideas.

'Go to sleep,' he advised his daughter thoughtfully before switching off the light and going downstairs.

He only wished he could go to bed himself, but he had some paperwork to do. The landscaping business, which he had built up from nothing, had thrived—two years running he had won critical acclaim from the judges at the Chelsea Flower Show and he was now fully booked up with design commissions for the next eighteen months.

Add to that the garden centre side of his business and it was no wonder that, increasingly, he was finding it difficult to juggle all the various demands on his time.

It had hurt him more than he liked to think about even now when Verity had made it plain that taking over from her uncle in his business meant more to her than being with him—had *hurt* him and had damn near *destroyed* him. It wasn't that he was arrogant enough to think that a woman, his woman, should not want to have a career or run her own life, it was just... It was just that he had assumed that their relationship, their love, had meant as much to her as it had to him and that...

Plainly, though, he had been wrong.

'Give me time,' she had begged him, and because he had loved her so much he had.

'I have to go to New York,' she had told him. 'But I'll be back... It won't be for ever and there'll be holidays.' But too many months had come and gone without her coming back and in the end he had been the one to go to her. A meagre forty-eight hours was all they had had together—all he'd been able to afford to pay for and he had only managed that because he had picked up the short break as a special tour operator's bargain.

'Don't make me wait too long,' he had begged her.

'Please understand,' she had asked him.

Finally, pushed to the limits of his pride and his love, he had given her an ultimatum.

'Come home, we need to talk,' he had written to her, but she had ignored his letter—and when he had rung her apartment a strange male voice had answered the phone, claiming not to know where she was.

He hadn't rung again and then, four weeks later, he had met Sarah, and the rest, as they said, was history.

The local paper had carried several articles about Verity's uncle five years ago when he had died—he had been, after all, probably the town's most successful and wealthy inhabitant—but Silas had never expected that Verity would come back.

If it hadn't been for that incident with Honor and her roller blades, he doubted that they would even have seen one another. And he wished to God that they hadn't. Tonight had resurrected too many painful memories. Grimly he switched his thoughts back to the present.

He was going to have to find someone to take care of Honor tomorrow. But who? He had used up all his credit with his normal 'babysitters'. If worse came to worst, he would have to take her to the garden centre with him and ask Anna to keep an eye on her.

He groaned. Sometimes she made him feel as old as Methuselah, and at others her maturity filled him with both awe and apprehension.

Earlier this evening, walking into the restaurant and seeing her there with Verity, he had felt such a confusing and powerful mixture of emotions and when they had both looked at him, identical womanly expressions of hauteur and dismissal in their eyes, he had felt, he had felt... Grimly he pushed his hand into his hair. They certainly made a formidable team.

A team... Oh, no. No! No! No way. No way...

Silas looked enquiringly at Honor as she replaced the telephone receiver as he walked into the kitchen.

She looked enviably fresh and alert in view of how late it had been when she had finally gone to bed last night.

'I've just checked with Verity,' she told Silas with a very grown-up air as she poured herself some cereal, 'and she says it's okay for me to stay with her today. I've arranged for her to come and collect me at ten o'clock.'

Silas opened his mouth and then closed it again and, going to make himself a cup of coffee, waited until he had poured the boiling water on the coffee grains before trusting himself to speak.

'Correct me if I'm wrong, Honor,' he began pleasantly, 'but I rather thought that *I* was the adult in this household and that as such *I* am the one who makes the decisions.'

'I knew you probably wouldn't have time to drive me over to Verity's,' Honor told him virtuously, 'that's why I asked *her* if she could come *here* to pick me up.'

'Honor!' Silas warned and then cursed under his breath as the phone rang.

By the time he had dealt with the call, Honor had made a strategic retreat to her bedroom.

The phone rang again as he snatched a quick gulp of his now cold coffee. Sooner rather than later he and Honor were going to have a serious talk—a *very* serious talk.

Honor waited until her father had gone out, leaving her in the temporary care of their cleaning lady, before making her second call of the morning.

'It's me,' she announced when she heard her friend Catherine pick up the receiver. 'Guess what?'

'Is it working?' Catherine asked her excitedly. 'Did your father…did they…?'

'Both of them are pretending that they've never met before,' Honor told her friend. 'I haven't told them about finding that photograph. I got Verity to take me out for supper last night like we planned—to the same place where Dad was taking Myra. You should have seen her face…'

'What, Verity's? Did she look as though she still loved him? Did he—'

'No, not *Verity*,' Honor interrupted her. 'I meant you should have seen *Myra's* face—she was furious.'

'I bet she wasn't too pleased later when your dad got that phone call about the garden centre being broken into either.' Catherine giggled.

'Mmm…that worked really well. Tell your cousin I'll pay him what I owe him when I get more pocket money. I can't stay on the phone too long. Verity's coming round for me at ten.

I'm spending the day with her. When she gets here we're going to do some womanly bonding.'

'What's that?' Catherine asked her uncertainly.

'I'm not sure, I read about it in a magazine. I think it's when you sit round and talk about babies and things,' Honor told her grandly.

'Oh. I'd rather talk about the boys,' Catherine informed her. 'Are you sure that your dad's still in love with her?'

'Positive. Last night they were kissing,' Honor informed her smugly.

'What? Did you see them?'

'No, but Dad had got lipstick on his mouth.'

'It could have been Myra's...'

'No. Myra wears red. This was pink...'

'But if they really love one another like you told me, how come he married your mother?'

'I don't know. I suppose they must have fallen out. Just think, if I hadn't found that photograph I'd never have discovered Dad and Verity knew each other before. I can't wait for them to get married.'

'Will you be a bridesmaid?' Catherine asked her wistfully.

'I'll be *the* bridesmaid,' Honor responded firmly, unaware of a touch of wistfulness in her voice too.

'They'll go away on one of those honeymoon things and leave you at home,' Catherine warned her, retaliating for Honor's comment about being 'the' bridesmaid and squashing her own hopes of wafting down the aisle alongside her friend in a cloud of pink tulle. Despite all Honor's chivvying, Catherine still retained regrettable fondness for their shared Barbie days.

'My uncle left Charlie at home when *he* re-married.'

'No, they won't,' Honor said adding, 'Verity would never let Dad leave me behind. She's so exactly right.' She smiled happily. 'I could tell the moment I met her.'

Catherine knew from experience when her friend's mind was on other things.

'I've got a new video,' she told her. 'We could watch it together on Saturday…'

'Maybe,' Honor hedged. 'I might not be very well…'

'Not very well? What do you mean?' Catherine demanded.

'Wait and see,' Honor responded mysteriously, before adding quickly, 'Verity's just driven up, I've got to go…'

'Daddy said to say thank you very much for looking after me,' Honor told Verity in a serious tone when she had opened the front door to her. 'He said he was very, very grateful to you and he couldn't think of anyone he could trust more to look after me.'

Verity blinked. To say she had been surprised to receive a telephone call from Honor asking if she could possibly spend the day with her because she was off school and Silas had to go out was something of an understatement. After what had happened between them last night she would have thought that *she* was the last person Silas would want around his daughter—and around himself.

What kind of a father *was* he exactly, if he could so easily entrust his only child to a woman he himself did not even pretend to like? she wondered critically as Honor skipped off to collect her coat.

Thoughtfully she waited for Honor to return.

'Your father *does* know that you're spending the day with me, doesn't he?' she questioned her dryly.

Honor gave her an injured look.

'Of course he does. You can ring him on his mobile if you like…'

'No. It's all right,' Verity assured her, adding palliatively, 'I'm not used to looking after little…*young* women… What would you like to do?'

'Could you take me shopping?' Honor asked her. 'I don't have any nice clothes,' she confided. 'Dad isn't very good at buying me the right kind of things. She looked down at her jeans and tee shirt and told Honor, 'I think sometimes he forgets that I'm a girl.'

Honor couldn't have said anything more guaranteed to touch her own heart, Verity ac-

knowledged. She too had suffered from hope-
lessly inaccurate male assessment of what kind
of clothes were suitable for a young girl.

Even so…

'Your father…' she began uncertainly, but
Honor shook her head.

'Dad won't mind,' she answered Verity excitedly. 'He'll be pleased. He *hates* taking me
shopping. In fact…' She paused and gave
Verity an assessing look, wondering how far
she should try her luck. Not too far if that unexpectedly shrewd question Verity had asked
her earlier was anything to go by. 'Well, he
has been saying that he would have to try and
find someone—a woman—to take me out
shopping.' Honor gazed up pleadingly at
Verity.

'Wouldn't Myra…?' Verity began cautiously.

But Honor immediately shook her head and
pulled a face before informing Verity tremulously, 'Myra doesn't like me… I think she…if
she ever married my father, she would try to
send me away…'

The horrified look Verity gave her reassured Honor. Everything was going to work out. Verity was going to make the *perfect* mother for her.

Prior to receiving Honor's telephone call Verity had planned to spend the day working, and a couple of hours after she had picked Honor up she was beginning to wonder if working might not have proved to be the easier option.

They were in the pre-teen department of a well-known chain of clothes shops, Verity waiting outside the cubicle area whilst Honor tried on the clothes she had chosen.

'And I thought having *teenagers* was bad,' another woman standing next to Verity groaned. 'My youngest...' she nodded in the direction of one of the changing rooms '...isn't speaking to her father because he refused to allow her to have her navel pierced. She's eleven next week. So far, the only clothes she's said she'll wear are the ones that her father will have forty fits if he sees her in, and I've got to admit he does have a point. Of course, we all know that fathers don't like to see their little girls growing up, but—'

'Verity, what do you think?' Honor demanded, suddenly emerging from the changing cubicle dressed in a tiny cut-off top that clung lovingly to her mercifully still flat chest and a pair of stretch Lycra leggings in a mixture of colours that made Verity's eyeballs ache.

'It's... I don't think your father will like it very much,' Verity began.

But she was out-manoeuvred as Honor informed her sunnily, 'No, I don't suppose he will, but you'll soon be able to talk him round.'

She could talk him round? Verity opened her mouth and then closed it again.

'Honor...' she began, but Honor was already disappearing in the direction of the changing cubicle.

It was another three hours before Honor pronounced herself reasonably satisfied with her purchases, declaring that she was hungry and suggesting that they made their way to the nearest McDonald's.

They were settled at a table when Honor asked Verity her most searching question yet. 'Have you ever been in love?'

Verity put down her cup of coffee.

'Once,' she admitted quietly, after a few long seconds had passed. 'A good many years ago.'

'What happened?' Honor asked her curiously.

Verity focused on her. What on earth was she *doing*? This wasn't a suitable topic of conversation to have with a ten-year-old girl even when the girl was the daughter of the man she had loved—especially when that ten-year-old was the daughter of the man she had loved, she corrected herself quickly—and yet, to her consternation, she still heard herself saying huskily, 'He...He married someone else!'

'Perhaps he married someone else because *he* thought *you'd* stopped loving him,' Honor told her quickly. 'Perhaps he really still loves you,' she said eagerly.

Verity started to frown. It was quite definitely time to change the subject.

'It's half past four,' she told Honor. 'What time did you say your father would be back?'

Silas' meeting had ended a little earlier than he had anticipated, and since he needed petrol he headed for the large out-of-town supermarket where he normally did his grocery shopping.

Catherine's mother was heading for the checkout with a full trolley-load when he walked in. Smiling at him, she asked, 'Did your aunt enjoy seeing Honor? Catherine was disappointed that she couldn't stay with us after all.'

Silas frowned.

'I'm sorry?' he began and then checked. What exactly was going on? Honor had told *him* that she couldn't stay at Catherine's because her friend had family visiting, but from what Catherine's mother had just said she seemed to be under the impression that it was *Honor* who had had the family commitment.

'Oh, and thanks for the invitation to dinner next week, we'd love to come.'

The invitation to dinner…? Next week? Silas opened his mouth and then closed it again. His daughter, he decided grimly, was going to have some serious explaining to do.

It was five o'clock when Verity finally pulled into Silas' drive, empty thankfully of his car, but she knew she couldn't escape until he returned home to care for his daughter. Besides, Honor was not feeling very well.

'My stomach hurts,' she told Verity.

'I'm not surprised. You *did* have two milk shakes,' Verity reminded her.

'It's not that kind of pain,' Honor came back quickly. 'It's the kind you get when you feel sad and…and lonely.'

Once they were inside the house, though, Honor suddenly remembered something she had to do outside.

'You stay here,' she told Verity, pushing open the kitchen door. 'I won't be long.'

The kitchen was generously proportioned and comfortable. In the adjoining laundry room Verity could see a basket perched on top of the tumble-dryer, a pile of clean laundry next to it as though someone had pulled it from the machine and not had time to fold it.

Automatically she walked through and started to smooth out the crumpled garments. Honor's underwear and school clothes and...

Her fingers tensed as she picked up a pair of soft male briefs, white and well styled. Her hands were trembling so much she almost dropped them. Quickly she put them down as though they had scalded her. She could hear Honor coming back.

'*I* bought Dad those for Christmas,' she told Verity, picking up the briefs.

'I'm learning to cook at school. You should have dinner parties and invite people round.'

Verity looked at her.

'Dinner parties?' she questioned warily.

'Mmm... Catherine's mother has them all the time. Dad was saying last week how embarrassed *he* felt because he wants to invite them round here but he doesn't have anyone to help him. I mean, he's okay really with the food, but it's the other things, isn't it?' Honor asked her earnestly. 'The flowers and the…the placements. Myra says that those are very important.'

The placements. Verity bit her inner lip to keep her mouth straight. It would never do to laugh and hurt Honor's feelings. The last time she had heard someone referring to the importance of their placements had been at a stuffy Washington diplomatic dinner.

'Er…yes,' she agreed. 'Well, I'm sure that Myra would be only too pleased to act as hostess for your father.'

'She can't,' Honor told her quickly, 'It's…Catherine's mother doesn't like her… Perhaps you could do it?' Honor suggested.

Verity's eyes widened.

'Me? But…'

'I don't know how well you can cook, but I could help.'

Verity automatically continued to fold the laundry. Now she stopped and turned to Honor.

'Honor,' she began gently, 'I don't think—'

'Dad's back, I just heard the car,' Honor interrupted her, adding quickly, 'Don't say anything to him about the dinner party... He doesn't like people thinking that he can't do things.'

Outside the kitchen door Silas hesitated. Just the sight of Verity's BMW had raised his heartbeat. What the hell was the matter with him? Hadn't he learned his lesson the *first* time around? Eleven years ago Verity had rejected him in favour of her uncle's business and he was a fool if he allowed himself to forget that fact.

Even so, the sight that met his eyes when he finally pushed open the kitchen door was one that made him check and curl his hand into a hard warning fist. Verity and Honor were standing in the laundry room deep in conversation, Honor holding the end of the sheet that Verity was busily folding.

'Dad always says that it's a waste of time to iron them because no one but us ever sees them.'

No one! Verity's heart gave a quick thud. Did that mean that Myra and he…? Or was it simply that he discreetly chose not to share a bed with his lover in the same house where his daughter slept?

'Dad!' Honor cried, releasing the sheet as she saw her father and bounding across the kitchen to hug him with such very evident love that Verity's heart gave another and even more painful lurch.

It was so obvious, watching the two of them together, not just that Honor was Silas' daughter but also how much they loved one another. There was nothing false or artificial about the way Silas held his daughter.

'Thank you for helping out,' he told Verity formally. 'I—'

'Dad, Verity took me shopping. Just wait until you see what we bought. I told her you'd pay her,' Honor hurried on, 'but she still wouldn't let me have some of the things I wanted. There was this top and these leggings…' She began enthusiastically explaining the eye-popping ensemble to Silas before adding, 'But Verity didn't think they were my colours.'

Over her head Silas' eyes met Verity's.

Thank you, he mouthed silently before turning his attention back to Honor and telling her gravely, 'I'm sure she was right.'

'Well, that's what I thought because her own clothes are so beautiful,' Honor agreed. 'Don't you think she looks luscious in that suit, Dad?'

Luscious…

Verity could feel her face starting to grow warm as two identical pairs of eyes studied her Donna-Karan-clad body.

'She certainly looks very…elegant…and successful,' Silas agreed quietly. But somehow, instead of sounding like a compliment, the words sounded much more like condemnation, Verity recognised grimly.

'I was just telling Verity how much you want to have a dinner party,' Honor chattered on, apparently oblivious to the tension growing between the two silent adults. 'She said she'd

love to come and help you and it will help her
to get to know people as well, won't it?'

'Honor…'

As they both spoke at once, Verity and Silas
looked at one another.

'Now you're both cross with me…'

Bright tears shimmered in Honor's hurt eyes
as her bottom lip wobbled and she turned her
head away.

Verity was immediately filled with guilt and
contrition. Out of her own embarrassment and
reluctance to have Silas think that she was deliberately inveigling her way back into his life,
she had inadvertently hurt Honor.

Silas looked less concerned but he was still
frowning.

'This dinner party,' he began, ignoring his
daughter's tear-filled eyes. 'It wouldn't be the
same one that Catherine's mother informed me
she would be delighted to attend, when I
bumped into her in the supermarket earlier,
would it, Honor?'

Honor gave him a sunny smile.

'Oh, can they come? Good... Catherine's mother is a brilliant cook,' she informed Verity, 'and—'

'Honor!' Silas began warningly.

Quickly Verity picked up her handbag.

'I think I'd better go,' she announced quietly.

'Go? Oh, no, not yet. I wanted you to stay for supper,' Honor pleaded.

'I'm afraid I can't... I... I have another appointment,' Verity fibbed.

Honor's eyes widened.

'But this afternoon you said that you were staying in tonight by yourself,' she reminded Verity in a confused little voice.

'I'll see you out,' Silas told her, shooting Honor a quelling look.

'Thank you once again for looking after Honor,' he told Verity formally as he accompanied her politely to her car.

Verity daredn't allow herself to look at him but suddenly he was striding past her, examining the front wheel of her car.

'You've got a flat tyre,' he told her sharply.

Disbelievingly Verity looked at her car.

'I...I've got a spare,' she told him, but he was shaking his head,

'*That* won't do much good,' he said curtly. 'The back one's flat as well. They've both got nails in them,' he informed her. 'You must have driven over them.'

'Yes, I must,' Verity agreed, shaking her head. 'But I don't know where. If I could use your phone to ring a garage...'

'You can, but I doubt you'll be able to get it fixed until the morning,' he told her dryly. 'It's more likely the garages round here will all be shut now.'

Helplessly Verity studied her now immobile car. How on earth had she managed to run over two nails—and where? She certainly hadn't been aware of doing so, nor of driving anywhere where she might have expected loose nails to be lying on the ground.

'Let's go back inside. I know the local dealer, I'll give him a ring,' Silas suggested.

Silently Verity followed Silas back into the house.

Watching them from the sitting-room window, Honor surreptitiously crossed her fingers. So far, so good—the plan to get them together was working beautifully. It had been hard work driving those nails into the tyres, though—much harder than she had expected.

'You *can't* do that,' Catherine had protested, her eyes widening in a mixture of shock and excitement when Honor had told her what she had planned to do.

'Watch me,' Honor had challenged her, bravado covering her brief twinge of guilt at what she had to do.

Verity waited in the kitchen with Honor whilst Silas went into his study to ring the garage. When he came back his expression was grave.

'The garage can't come out until tomorrow, I'm afraid, which means that you're going to have to spend the night here.'

Verity opened her mouth to protest and say that if he couldn't run her home she could get a taxi, and then, for some inadmissible and dangerous reason, she found that she was closing it again.

'Oh, good, now we can play Scrabble and you can share my bedroom,' Honor was saying excitedly.

'Verity can sleep in the guest bedroom,' Silas reproved crisply, 'and as for Scrabble—'

Verity smiled. Honor had told her earlier in the day how much she enjoyed the game.

'I'd love to play with her,' she interrupted Silas pacifically, adding truthfully, 'It's always been one of my favourite games.'

'Yes. I... I enjoy it as well,' Silas agreed.

Her heart hammering too fast for comfort, Verity wondered if that slight hesitation in his voice had been her imagination. Had he, as she had momentarily felt, been about to say that he remembered how much she had enjoyed Scrabble?

Ridiculous to feel such a warm, fuzzy, sentimental, inappropriate surge of happiness at the thought.

'I still can't understand where I managed to pick up those nails,' Verity commented, shaking her head.

They had just cleared away after supper and Honor had gone upstairs to get the Scrabble.

'Where they came from is immaterial now,' Silas pointed out. 'The damage is done...'

'Mmm...'

'More wine?' Silas offered her, picking up the still half-full bottle from the kitchen table.

On the point of refusing, Verity changed her mind. What harm could it do, after all, and since she wasn't driving...? The meal they had eaten had been a simple one of chicken and vegetables, prepared by Silas with Honor's rather erratic assistance.

It had touched Verity, though, when Honor had insisted on dragging her out to the garden with her so that they could find some flowers to put on the table.

'Dad, when you have the dinner party, you'll have to use the dining room,' she told her father whilst they were eating. 'I'll show you the dining room afterwards, Verity,' she informed Verity with a woman-to-woman look. 'You'll need to know where everything is.'

'Honor,' Silas began, 'I don't think—'

But Honor refused to listen to him, turning instead to Verity and demanding passionately, 'You will do it, won't you, Verity? Please,' before telling her father, 'You don't understand... I *hate* it at school when the others talk about the parties their mothers give. I can tell that they're all feeling sorry for me. I know that Verity may not be able to cook, but *we* can have just as good a dinner party here as they have.'

After such a passionate outburst, what else could Verity do other than swallow her own feelings and give in? Silas, she suspected, must be swallowing equally hard—harder, perhaps, if the frowning look on his face was anything to go by.

'You had no business inviting Catherine's mother and father round, though, no matter the circumstances...' Pausing, Silas shook his head before adding sternly, 'No business at all. But since you *have*, I agree that we can hardly tell Catherine's mother the truth. Please don't

feel that *you* have to get involved, though—'
he told Verity.

'I'd be happy to help,' Verity cut him off,
looking him straight in the eye as she told him
quietly, 'I know how Honor feels, but, of
course, if there's someone else you would pre-
fer to act as your hostess…?'

She waited. Would he tell her that, by rights,
Myra ought to be the one hostessing his dinner
party? And what if he did? Why should that
concern *her*?

'No. There's no one,' he denied before adding, 'Besides, this will be *Honor's* dinner
party, I suspect, not mine…'

'You can choose the wine, Dad,' Honor informed him in a kind voice. 'That's the man's
job. What will we do about food?' she asked
Verity excitedly.

'We'll sort something out,' Verity promised
her whilst she mentally reviewed which of her
favourite dishes she should serve.

In London she had had little time for giving
dinner parties, but when she had they had been
occasions she had thoroughly enjoyed.

Good food, good wine and good friends—most of all good friends; they were a recipe for the very best kind of entertaining. But she didn't know Silas' friends and the situation was bound to be both uncomfortable and awkward. He was being polite about it now, just as he had been good-mannered about the accident to her tyres and the fact that he had been forced to offer her a bed for the night. But they both knew how he really felt about her.

Quickly now, Verity reached for her wine and took a deep gulp, grimacing a little as the wine's sharpness hit her palate.

'You never did have much of a head for alcohol,' Silas commented, watching her.

Silently their glances met and held.

'That was over ten years ago,' Verity finally managed to tell him huskily. 'My…tastes have changed since then.'

'Here it is…'

Both of them looked round as Honor came bounding into the room carrying the Scrabble.

CHAPTER SEVEN

'RIGHT, time for bed...'

'Oh, Dad, just *one* more game,' Honor protested, but Silas was already shaking his head.

'You said that last time,' he reminded her sternly.

Diplomatically Verity busied herself tidying up the letters and putting everything away. Honor had needed no allowances made for her and she had thoroughly trounced them, not once, but twice—perhaps because in Verity's own case, at least, her concentration had been more on the words that Honor had formed than matching them, she admitted, quickly glancing away from Honor to the board.

Love... Tiff... Quarrel... Mama... Surely she was being over-sensitive in her reaction to seeing those words? After all, Honor knew nothing about the past, their shared past.

Quickly Verity broke up the words and folded the board.

'You will come up and say goodnight to me, won't you?' Honor begged Verity, adding determinedly, 'I want you both to come up... together...'

Verity couldn't bring herself to look at Silas. Instead she went to wash the empty coffee mugs whilst Silas took Honor upstairs.

She was just about to remove their wineglasses when he came back down.

'No, leave those,' he told her. 'We might as well finish off the bottle.'

'I'll just go up and say goodnight to Honor,' Verity told him huskily.

Standing in the kitchen on her own whilst he'd been upstairs with Honor had given her too much time to think, to remember...to regret...

If things had been different Honor could have been *her* child... If things had been different... If Silas had not rejected her... If... If... But what use were 'ifs'? No use whatsoever to an aching, lonely, yearning heart. A heart that still beat ridiculously fast for a man who had hurt it so badly.

Honor was lying flat beneath the bedclothes, her hair a dark mass on the pillow. Automatically as she bent to kiss her Verity smoothed it back off her face.

'I do like you, Verity,' Honor told her softly. 'I wish you could be here with us for always…'

Sharp tears pricked Verity's eyes. She wasn't totally gullible, and she was perfectly well aware that Honor wasn't averse to using soft soap and flattery to get her own way, but for once there was no mistaking the very real emotion in the little girl's voice. The real emotion and the real need, Verity recognised.

Honor was looking, if not for a mother, then certainly for a mentor, a role model, a woman with whom she could bond. None knew better than she herself just how it felt to be on the verge of young womanhood without any guiding female influence in one's life, Verity acknowledged. It was one of the loneliest and most isolated places on earth—almost as lonely and heartache inducing as being without the man you had given your heart to.

Her uncle, although providing for her material welfare, had been oblivious to the emotional needs of a young girl, and Verity remembered with painful clarity how she as a young adolescent had tried desperately to attach herself to the mother of a school friend, and then, when that had been gently discouraged by the woman in question, she had turned instead to one of her schoolteachers. But both women, although kind and caring, had had their own families and their own lives, and their distancing of themselves from her had left Verity feeling even more bereft than before— and not just bereft, but sensitively aware of being gently held at a distance.

Honor, she suspected, although on the surface a very different girl from the one she had been, was going through a similar stage. There was no doubting Silas' love for his daughter, nor his caring paternal concern for her. He was, Verity could see, a father who was very actively involved in his daughter's life, but

Honor was making it plain that she wanted a *woman's* influence in her life as well as her father's.

'You will stay the night, won't you?' she whispered now, clutching Verity's hand. 'I want you to be here when I wake up in the morning...'

'I'll be here,' Verity promised her.

'I like your hair best when it's down,' Honor told her sleepily. 'It makes you look...more huggy. Catherine, my friend, has got two brothers and loads and loads of cousins...' Her eyes closed. Very gently, Verity bent and kissed her.

For all her outer layer of sturdy independence, inside she was still very much a little girl. Silas' little girl.

Quietly Verity got up and headed for the bedroom door.

Alone in the kitchen, Silas allowed himself to relax for the first time since he had come home. He didn't know what kind of game Honor thought she was playing by inveigling

Verity into agreeing to hosting that damned dinner party, and the only reason he hadn't given her a thorough dressing down over it was because he was well aware that she had reached that sensitive and delicate stage in her development where her burgeoning pride and sense of self could be very easily bruised. He would have to talk to her about it, of course, and explain that she had put Verity in a very embarrassing and difficult position.

It had been hard to guess exactly what Verity's real feelings about the situation were. She had developed a disconcerting, calm, distancing and very womanly maturity which, very effectively, drew a line over which no one was allowed to cross, but he certainly knew how he was going to feel, sitting at the opposite end of the dining table from her whilst she acted as his hostess. It was going to be sheer hell, total purgatory, an evening filled with excruciating pain of 'could have beens' and all because his darling daughter wanted to be on a par with her school friends.

Well, he couldn't blame her for that. It was all part and parcel of growing up. Honor was getting ready to grow into womanhood and she was making it clear to him that she wanted a woman in her life to pattern herself on.

He had, at one stage, wondered if Myra— but the pair of them would never accept one another.

Had Verity been anyone other than who she was he suspected that by now he would have been thanking fate for bringing her into their lives. It was glaringly obvious how Honor felt about her—and not just from the determined way she was attaching herself to Verity. If he was honest with himself, which he always tried to be, without the past to cast its unhappy shadow he knew perfectly well that, had he been meeting Verity for the first time now, he would have been instantly and immediately attracted to her.

She had still, despite the life she had lived, an air of soft and gentle femininity, an aura of natural womanly strength melded with compassion and love.

He found it hard to picture her as the head of a multi-million-pound business making corporate decisions based purely on profits and completely without emotion. It wasn't that he doubted her skills or abilities, it was just that, to him, even now, she still possessed that certain something that made him want to look after her and protect her.

Protect her? Was he crazy? She *had* all the protection she needed in the shape of the material assets she had chosen above their love.

'It's my duty, I owe it to him,' she had told him sadly when she had allowed her uncle to part them and send her away to New York, but those had been words he hadn't wanted to hear.

Last night, holding her in his arms, kissing her... She'd been back less than a week and already... He wasn't going to make the same mistake he had made last time. This time he was going to be on his guard and stay on it...

He had known, of course, of her uncle's plans for Verity's future and the way her uncle had deliberately fostered and used her strong sense of duty for his own ends.

One of the first things he had decided when he had found himself widowed and the father of a baby girl was that he would never ever manipulate her feelings and cause her to feel that she was in debt to him for anything in the way he had witnessed Verity's uncle manipulating hers.

But, naively perhaps, he had assumed that Verity had shared his feelings, his belief that their future lay together.

'Do you love me?' he had demanded, and shyly she had nodded.

Had she ever loved him or…?

'I'll be back soon from New York and then…then we can be together,' she told him.

And he had taken that to mean that she had wanted to marry him, and share his dream of establishing a business together.

He could still remember the sense of excitement and pride he had felt the day he had first taken her to see the small run-down market garden he had hoped to buy. She had seemed as thrilled and excited as him.

'There's a real market locally for a garden centre and a landscaping service, but it won't be easy,' he warned her. 'I've been through all the figures with the bank and for the first few years we're going to have to plough back every penny we make into the business. I won't be able to buy us a big house or give you a nice car.'

'I don't care about things like that,' Verity assured him softly, making one of those lightning changes she could make from a girl's *naïveté* to a woman's maturity and shaking his heart to its roots in the process. It fascinated and delighted him, held him in thrall with awe to be privileged to see these glimpses of the woman she was going to be. She was so gentle, so loving, so everything that most appealed to him in a woman.

'I don't care where we live just so long as we're together...'

'Well, I should certainly make enough to support a wife and our child, our children...'

he had whispered. It was all he wanted then. His parents were away on holiday with friends and he took her home with him, making love to her in the warm shadows of the summer evening. He was twenty-seven and considered himself already a man; she was twenty-one.

'I'm going to see the bank manager tomorrow,' he whispered to her as he slowly licked and then kissed her pretty pink fingertips, 'and then I'm going to put a formal offer in on the business. Once it's ours, we can start to make plans for our wedding.'

He thought that the quick tears that filled her eyes were tears of love and pleasure—she often wept huge silent tears of bliss after their lovemaking—and it was only later that he realised that she had wept because she had known that, by the time he was the owner of the small plot of land, she would be on the other side of the Atlantic.

Silas warned her repeatedly that her uncle was trying to separate them, that he had his own selfish reasons for not wanting them to marry, but Verity refused to listen.

Her uncle wasn't like that, she protested, white-faced. He didn't push the matter, thinking he knew how vulnerable she was, how much she needed to believe that the man who had brought her up did care more about her than his business, not wanting to do anything that might potentially hurt her.

Hurt her! Did *she* care about hurting *him* when she ignored his letter, his pleas to her to come home? She didn't even care enough to write to him and tell him that it was over. She simply ignored his letter.

And then her uncle called round, supposedly to buy some plants but in reality to tell him that Verity had decided to stay on in New York for a further year.

The business wasn't building up as fast as Silas had expected. He was struggling to service the bank borrowing he had taken out to buy and develop the garden centre, and when his bank manager telephoned him a week later to inform him that they had had an anonymous offer from someone wanting to buy the newly established garden centre from him he was so tempted to take it, to move away and make a fresh start somewhere else. What, after all, was there to keep him in the area any longer? His parents had decided to retire to Portugal, and he knew there was no way he could bear to live in the same town as Verity once she *did* return to take over her uncle's business—but then fate stepped in, throwing him a wild card.

He had obtained tickets for the annual prestigious Chelsea Flower Show—two of them—because he had assumed by then that Verity would be back from New York and he had wanted to take her with him.

Almost, he decided not to go. He had lost his love, and it looked very much as if he could soon be losing his business as well, but the tickets were bought and paid for and so he set out for London.

He saw Sarah when he was booking in at his hotel. She was staying there too, a thin, too pale girl who looked nothing like Verity and whom, if he was honest, he felt more sympathy for than desire. Her attempts to pick him up were so obvious and awkward that he had took pity on her and offered to buy her a drink. She was, she told him, originally from Australia where she had lived with foster parents, and she had come to England trying to trace her birth mother.

Whilst living in London she had met and fallen in love with a fellow Australian who had now left the country to continue his round-the-world tour, refusing to take Sarah with him.

'I thought he loved me,' she told Silas sadly, 'but he didn't, he was just using me.'

Her words and her sadness struck a sombre chord within Silas. In an attempt to cheer her up he offered her his spare ticket for the flower show, which she accepted.

They spent all that day together and the next, although there was nothing remotely sexual between them. Silas simply didn't feel that way about her. Verity was the only woman he wanted. Emotionally he might hate her for what she had done to him, but physically, at night alone in his bed, he still ached and yearned for her.

Even now he still didn't know what prompted him to knock on Sarah's door the second night after they had met. She didn't answer his knock but when, driven by some sixth sense, he turned the handle and pushed open the door, he found her seated on the bed, a glass of water in one hand and a bottle of pills on the bed beside her.

He shook her so savagely as he demanded to know how many she had taken that it was a wonder her neck didn't snap, he acknowledged later.

'None,' she told him dull-eyed, 'not yet...'

'Not yet. Not ever!' Silas told her sharply, picking up the bottle and going through to the bathroom to flush the contents down the lavatory.

When he came back she was crying soullessly into her hands.

'Don't go,' she begged him. 'I don't want to be on my own.'

And so he stayed and, inevitably perhaps, they had sex, out of compassion and pity on his part and loneliness and need on hers.

In the morning they went their separate ways, but not before Silas had insisted on giving Sarah his telephone number and getting her own address from her.

He was concerned enough about her to telephone her as soon as he got home and to ring her regularly twice a week after that.

Always, at the back of his mind, was the concern that she might succumb and try a second time to take her own life. She had told him sadly that when her boyfriend had moved on she had felt she had nothing left to live for. His own pain at losing Verity had enabled him to understand what she had been feeling. He had counselled her to think about returning to Australia and her foster parents and friends, and she had promised him she would think about doing so, and then he received the tearful telephone call that was to completely change his life—to change both their lives.

She was pregnant, she told him, an accident. She was on the pill but had forgotten to take it. He was not to worry, she said, she intended to have the pregnancy terminated.

Silas reacted immediately and instinctively, taking the first train to York where she was living.

'I can't afford a baby,' she protested when he told her that he didn't want her to have a termination.

'This is *my* baby as well as yours,' Silas reminded her sombrely. 'We could get married and share the responsibility.'

'Get married? *Us*…? You and me? But you don't… It was just sex,' she protested shakily.

Just sex maybe, but they had still created a new life between them, and in the end she gave way and they were married very quickly and very quietly.

From the start Honor had been an independent, cheerful child. Until she had started school Silas had often taken her to work with him and the bond between them was very close and strong. She had asked about her mother, of course, and Silas had told her what little he knew, but until recently she had always seemed perfectly happy for there just to be the two of them.

➥He had named her Honor as a form of promise to Sarah that he would always honour the bargain they had made between them to put the welfare of the child they had created first, and he believed that he had always honoured that bargain.

He could hear Verity coming back downstairs now.

'I… I'm sorry about…about the car…' she told him awkwardly as she walked into the kitchen.

'It's hardly your fault,' Silas pointed out.

'Do you plan to stay in town long?' he asked her politely as he handed her the glass of wine he had poured her.

'I… I'm not really sure yet.'

Silas frowned. 'Surely the business—?' he began, but Verity cut him off, shaking her head.

'I sold it… It was either that or risk being forcibly taken over. I plan to use the money to establish a charitable trust in my uncle's name,' she told him.

Silas fought hard not to let his shock show. What had happened to the woman who had put the business before their love? Verity must have changed dramatically—or perhaps weakened. Quickly he caught himself up. There was no point in allowing his thoughts to travel down *that* road, or in hoping, *wishing*—what? That she had had such a change of heart earlier, that their love…that he had been more important to her, that they could have… Stop it, he warned himself.

'It must have been hard for you, making the decision to sell,' he commented as unemotionally as he could. 'After all, it's been your life…'

Her *life*. Had he any idea how cruel he was being? Verity wondered. Did he know what it did to her to be told by him, of all people, that her life was so cold and empty and lacking in real emotion? She stiffened her spine and put down her glass.

'No more than *your* business has been yours,' she pointed out quietly.

It wasn't true, of course—his work had been something that he loved, that he had chosen *freely* for himself, whilst hers... Not even with him could she be able to discuss how it had felt to finally step out from beneath the heavy burden that the business had always been to her, to feel free, to be her own person for the first time in her life.

Verity drew in her breath with a small hiss of pain.

'I think I'd like to go to bed,' she told him shakily. 'It's been a long day.'

Meaning, of course, that she didn't want to spend any time with him, Silas recognised.

'I'll take you up,' he told her curtly.

The guest room, Verity discovered, was more of a small, private suite on the top floor of the house in what must have originally been the attics—a pretty, good-sized bedroom with sloping ceiling and its own bathroom plus a small sitting room.

'I had this conversion done for Honor,' Silas informed her. 'She's getting to an age where she needs her own space and her own privacy.'

As he turned and walked towards the door Verity had a strong compulsion to run after him and stop him.

'Silas...'

He stopped and turned round, waiting in silence.

'Goodnight,' she told him shakily.

'Goodnight,' he returned.

After showering and brushing her hair, Verity crept into bed. It felt so strange being here in Silas' house. During the years they had been apart she had resisted the temptation to think about Silas and what might have been. She thought she had learnt to live with the pain, but seeing him again had reawakened not just the pain she had felt but all her other emotions as well. She couldn't possibly still love him. Hadn't she learned her lesson? Verity could feel the back of her throat beginning to ache with the weight of her suppressed tears as she closed her eyes and willed herself to go to sleep.

CHAPTER EIGHT

SILAS woke up abruptly. There was a sour taste in his mouth from the wine he had drunk and his head ached. Swinging his legs out of bed, he stood up and reached for his robe. His weight was much the same now as it had always been but his body was far more heavily muscled than it had been when he was in his twenties—the work he did was responsible for that, of course. Shaking his head, he padded barefoot out onto the landing and into the bathroom. He needed a glass of water.

He was just reaching into the bathroom cabinet for an aspirin when he heard a familiar sound. Putting down the glass of water he had been holding, he walked quickly towards Honor's door. When she was younger she had often woken in the night in tears, frightened by some bad monster disturbing her dreams, but when he gently opened her bedroom door she was sleeping deeply and peacefully.

Still frowning, he glanced towards the stairs that led to the guest suite.

The noise was clearer now, a soft, heart-tearing sobbing. Verity was crying?

Immediately, taking the stairs two at a time, Silas hurried to her room, pushing open the door.

Like Honor she was asleep, but unlike Honor her sleep wasn't peaceful. The bed-clothes were tangled and the duvet half off the bed, exposing the creamy softness of her skin. As he realised that, like him, she slept in the nude, Silas hastily willed himself to ignore the temptation to let his gaze stray to her body, concentrating instead on her pale, tear-stained face.

Without her make-up and with her hair down she looked no different now than she had done at nineteen and, for a moment, the temp-tation to gather her up in his arms and hold her close was so strong that he had to take a step back from the bed to prevent himself from doing so.

In her sleep Verity gave a small, heartbreaking little cry, fresh tears rolling down her face from her closed eyes.

Silas could remember how rarely she had cried, how brave and independent she had always tried to be. Once, when they had quarrelled about something—he had forgotten what, some minor disagreement—she had turned her face away from him in the car and he had thought she had been sulking until he had looked in the wing mirror and seen the tears streaming from her eyes.

'I didn't want you to see me cry,' she had told him when he had stopped the car and taken her in his arms. 'It hurts so much.'

'The last thing I want to do is hurt you,' Silas had told her and meant it.

In her sleep Verity was reliving the events of the final summer of her relationship with Silas. After the two days they had spent together, New York had seemed even more lonely than ever. The work she had been doing with her uncle's old friend had been mentally and physically demanding and yet, at the same time somehow, very unsatisfying. She hadn't got the heart for it, Verity had acknowledged. Her heart had been given to Silas. Just how empty her life had been without him had been brought home to her during the two days they had spent together. Then, she had felt alive, whole, complete… When he had gone… It had been less than a week since he had flown home, having begged her to tell her uncle that she had changed her mind and that her future now lay with Silas.

'I can't do it,' she protested.

'It's business, Verity,' Silas argued, 'that's all. *We're* human beings with feelings, needs… I miss you and I want us to be together.'

'I miss you too,' Verity told him.

Initially she had been supposed to be spending four months in New York, but the original four had stretched to eight and then twelve, and every time she mentioned coming home her uncle procrastinated and said that, according to his friend, there was a great deal she still had to learn.

Sometimes the temptation to tell him that she simply couldn't do what he wanted her to do was so strong that she almost gave in to it, and then she would remember how he had taken her in.

Although it had never been discussed between them, Verity had the feeling that her uncle blamed her for her father's death. He and her mother had been on their way to collect her from a birthday party she had insisted on going to when they had been involved in the fatal accident which had killed them both, and she felt as though, in taking his place, she was doing some kind of penance, making some kind of restitution.

She had tried to say as much to Silas but he always got so angry when they discussed her uncle that she had simply not been able to do so. And her uncle seemed to dislike and resent Silas as much as Silas did him.

'Have you any idea just how wealthy you are going to be?' he demanded of Verity when she begged him to allow her to return home. 'You must be very careful, Verity,' he warned her. 'There are always going to be hungry and ambitious men out there who will try to convince you that they love you. Don't listen to them.'

'Silas isn't like that,' she protested defensively.

'Isn't he?' her uncle countered grimly. 'Well, he is certainly a young man with an awful lot of debts—far too many to be able to support a wife.'

'Come home,' Silas begged her.

But she said, 'No...not until I have fulfilled my debt to my uncle.'

Shortly after Silas returned to England, the murder of one of her fellow tenants in the block where she rented an apartment resulted in her uncle insisting that she moved to a safer address.

Verity tried to telephone Silas to tell him that she was moving but, when she wasn't able to get any reply either from Silas' home telephone or the garden centre, she had to ask her uncle to pass on to him her new address and telephone number.

She knew from what Silas had told her during his visit that he had several new commissions and was working virtually eighteen hours a day, which explained why she was unable to get hold of him.

A month later when she had still not heard from him she finally made herself acknowledge the truth. She loved him and missed him—dreadfully. He was the most important thing, the most important person in her life, and even though it meant disappointing her uncle she knew that it was impossible for her to go on denying her feelings, her love, any longer. She wanted to go home.

She rang her uncle, who assured her that he had passed on to Silas her new address and telephone number.

Silas was angry and upset with her, Verity acknowledged. It had taken a lot for him to beg her to come home as he had done and, no doubt, she had hurt his pride when she had been unable to say yes.

She knew how little he had been able to afford either the time or the money for his spur-of-the-moment flying visit to her, and she wished she had been able to tell him then how much she was missing him and how much she wished she could be with him.

When another two months passed without him getting in touch with her, she finally acknowledged the truth. She had lost weight; she couldn't sleep; she thought about him night and day; she ached so badly for him that the pain of missing him was with her all the time. She loved him so much that, even if it meant letting her uncle down, she knew that it was impossible for her to go on denying her feelings. There must surely be a way that she could be with Silas and do as her uncle wished, a way she did not have to choose between them, but if there wasn't…

If there wasn't, then she had made up her mind, selfish though it might be: being with Silas was more important to her than pleasing her uncle. She wanted to go home; she wanted to be with Silas; she wanted to be held in his arms close to his heart; she wanted to hear him telling her in that gruff, sexy voice he used after they had made love that he loved her and needed her and that he would never ever let her go. She wanted to hear him telling her how much he wanted her to be his wife, how much he wanted them to spend their lives together.

Reliving the times they had had together over and over again in the empty loneliness of her apartment was no substitute for the reality of being with him.

Without giving herself time to change her mind, she booked herself on the first available flight home, without telling anyone what she was doing. She wanted to surprise Silas, to see the look in his eyes when she walked into his arms, to show him that he meant more to her than anything else, than anyone else, in the world.

Confronting her uncle wasn't going to be easy, she knew that. She was twenty-two, old enough to know her own mind and to make her own decisions.

She bought a copy of the local newspaper whilst she waited for a taxi to take her from the station to the garden centre. Without that, without seeing that small, bare announcement of Silas' marriage to another woman, she wouldn't have known, would have walked into a situation for which she was totally unprepared.

The taxi driver, seeing her white face, was concerned enough to ask her if she was ill.

Verity looked at him blankly, her gaze returning to the newsprint in front of her. Silas was *married*. How could that be possible? He had been going to marry *her*. Was she suffering from some kind of madness, some kind of delusion? Was it all just a bad dream? How *could* Silas be married to someone else? There must have been a mistake, and yet she knew that there was no mistake, just as she now knew the reason for his silence during these last long weeks.

The pain was like nothing she had ever imagined experiencing: a tearing, wrenching, soul-destroying agony that made her want to scream and howl and tear at herself and her clothes, to ease a grief she could neither control nor contain.

She made the taxi driver take her back to the station. *En route* to Heathrow and a transatlantic flight back to New York she couldn't understand why, despite the heat of the day, her fingers and toes felt as cold as ice, so cold that they hurt, her movements those of a very, very old woman.

Back in New York she applied herself to her work with a grim concentration, throwing up a barrier around herself that she would allow no one to pass through.

Silas hadn't loved her at all. Silas had lied to her. Her uncle was right. From now on she was going to devote herself to the business. What else, after all, was there for her?

Fresh tears rolled down Verity's face—the tears she had never allowed herself to cry during the reality of her heartbreak at losing Silas but which now, reliving those days in her sleep, she had no power to suppress.

Silas. Not even in the privacy of her apartment had she allowed herself the weakness of whispering his name, of reliving all the times they had shared together.

'Silas…'

As he heard her say his name Silas closed his eyes. It hurt him to hear the emotion in her voice and to see the evidence of the distress on her damp face.

Very gently he reached out and touched her wet cheek. Her skin felt cool beneath his fingertips, her eyelashes ridiculously long as they fanned darkly on her cheek. She was lying half on and half off the pillow and automatically he slid his hand beneath the nape of her neck intending to make her more comfortable, just as he often did for Honor. But Verity wasn't Honor, a child…his child… She was a woman…his woman…

The shudder that galvanised his body was its own warning but it was a warning that came far too late. He stiffened as Verity suddenly opened her eyes.

'Silas…'

The husky wonderment in her voice held him spellbound.

'Silas.'

She said his name again, breathing it as unsteadily as an uncertain swimmer gulping air. As she struggled to sit up, the duvet slid further from her body, leaving it clothed only in the soft silver moonlight coming in through the window.

Silas caught his breath. In her early twenties she had had the body of a girl, slender and gently curved, only hinting at what it would be in maturity, but now she was fully a woman, her curves were so richly sensuous that he had to close his eyes to stop himself from reaching out to touch her just to make sure that she was real. He could feel the beads of sweat beginning to pearl his skin as he was flooded with hungry desire for her.

Even though he had looked away immediately, every detail of her was already imprinted on his eyeballs and his emotions. His hands ached to cup the ripe softness of her breasts, to stroke the taut warmth of her belly, to cover the feminine crispness of her pubic curls, to...

The power of his reaction to her, not just sexually but emotionally as well, shocked him into immobility.

'Silas...'

Reluctantly he opened his eyes as she whispered his name. Her mouth looked soft and warm, her eyes confused and unhappy. He lifted his hand to touch her hair and let it slide silkily through his fingers, his body shuddering as he started to release her.

Verity watched wide-eyed, still caught up in the intensity of her dream, her glance following Silas' every movement. Pleadingly she raised her hand to touch the side of his face, her palm flat against his jaw where she could feel his beard prickling her skin.

Silas closed his eyes as he moaned her name, a tortured, haunted sound of denial, but Verity was too lost in what she was doing to respond to it. Her fingertips trembled as she pressed them against his mouth, exploring its familiar shape, feeling them move as he mouthed her name. Instinctively she slipped them between his lips.

Immediately her nipples hardened, the muscles in her belly and thighs tautening as she shook with the force of what she was feeling.

Helplessly Silas opened his mouth, his tongue tip caressing the smooth warmth of her fingertips. He could see as well as feel her whole body trembling in reaction to his caress. Holding her arm, he sucked slowly on her fingers.

Beneath her breath Verity made a small, familiar keening noise as she lifted her other hand to his face, stroking him with frantic little movements, far more sensual and exciting for all their lack of open sexuality than a more calculatedly sexual caress could ever have been.

His self-control breaking, Silas caught hold of her hands, bearing her back against the softness of the pillow, his hands now cupping her face as he started to kiss her, opening her mouth with his lips, his tongue, feeding rather than satisfying his hunger for her with passionate, deeply intimate kisses.

As she opened her mouth to him, Verity caught back a small sob of relief. It had been so awful, dreaming that she had lost Silas, but here he was, with her, holding her, loving her, showing her that she was safe.

The smell of him, the sight of him, the *feel* of him, totally overwhelmed her starved senses, her body, so sensitive to him that her breasts were aching for his touch even before she felt his hands reaching out to cup them. Eagerly she moved to accommodate and help him, shivering in mute pleasure as she felt the hard familiarity of his palms against the taut peaks of her nipples.

Beneath his robe he was naked and it was heaven to have the luxury of sliding her hands up over his shoulders and down his back, to feel the solid male warmth of his skin, his *body* beneath her hands, to have the longed-for male reality of his flesh against her own, to feel that she was totally and completely surrounded and protected by him.

'Silas.' As she said his name she moved beneath him, silently inviting him to increase the intimacy between them.

As he felt her lifting her body towards his Silas groaned. He could feel her trembling as he touched her and he knew that he was shaking just as much. There hadn't been this much sexual tension between them even the first time they had made love. It felt as though their bodies were waiting to explode, to meld, to come together so completely that they could never be parted again.

She felt so good, so right…so…so Verity. He wanted to touch her, kiss her, possess her so completely that she would never be able to leave him again.

His hand touched her stomach and she rose up eagerly against him. He bent his mouth towards her breast, holding his breath as he started to lick delicately at her nipple, half afraid he might accidentally hurt her as he forced himself to go slowly, but Verity seemed to have no such inhibitions, her hand going to the back of his head as she pulled him closer to her body so that his mouth opened fully over her damp nipple.

Shuddering, he drew it deeply into his mouth and started to suck rhythmically on her. Beneath his hand he could feel the flesh of her belly grow hot and damp. Her face was flushed with desire, her body trembling as she made small, pleading cries deep in her throat.

Wordlessly he parted her thighs. The room was light enough for him to be able to see her naked body, and her sex. He could remember how shy she had been the first time he had whispered to her how much he wanted to see her, to look at her. But she had still let him and he could still remember the sense of awe and love he had felt, knowing just how much she trusted him.

He could see that same trust in her eyes now and, even though he knew he was deluding himself, it was almost as though there had never been anyone else for her but him, as though her body had never known any other lover, as though it had memories of only him, his touch, his need, his love.

Sombrely he parted her soft outer lips, exposing the secret kernel of her sex. His heart was thudding frantically fast, his own body stiff with arousal and need. He could see her looking at him, silent and wide-eyed as she reached out to caress him with her fingertips.

Very gently he touched her, coaxing, caressing.

Verity gave a low, aching groan, her hand tightening around him. She could feel her body responding to him, aching for him. It had been without him for so long that it needed no preliminaries, hungry and eager now for the longed-for feel of him within it.

'I want you, Silas,' she told him jerkily. 'I need you…now… Oh, yes, now…' she whispered frantically. 'Now. Now…now…'

The rhythm of their lovemaking was fast and intense, their shared climax a juddering, explosive catalyst of release that left them both trembling as Silas held Verity in his arms.

'Stay with me,' Verity whispered to him as her exhausted body slid into sleep. 'Don't leave me, Silas. Please don't leave me... Not this time...'

As she slept Silas looked down into her face. She was a woman now, a woman with a woman's needs, a woman's sexuality. If she hadn't loved him enough to put their love first before, she was hardly likely to do so now. She might want him sexually, she might even stay for a while, but it wasn't just his own emotions she was likely to hurt this time, his own heart she could easily break. There was Honor to consider as well.

'Stay with me,' she had begged him. But she was the one who had left *him*. *She* was the one who had refused to stay.

Very slowly he eased himself away from her, picking up his discarded robe as he looked down at her.

'Stay with me,' she had said. As he bent and kissed her cheek a single tear rolled down her face, but it wasn't one of her own.

Clenching his jaw, Silas walked towards the door, closing it quietly behind him without daring to look back.

CHAPTER NINE

VERITY surfaced slowly from the deepest and most relaxing sleep she could remember having in a long time. She stretched luxuriously, a womanly knowing smile curling her mouth. Her body felt deliciously, blissfully satisfied. Even her skin where the sunlight shone warmly on her exposed arm on top of the duvet seemed to have a silken, sensuous shimmer to it. She closed her eyes and made a purring sound of female happiness deep in her throat as she savoured the novelty of feeling so good. It was as if she had opened a present, spilling out from it a glowing, sparkling, magical gift of happiness and love. Mmm... Her eyes still closed, she rolled over and reached out for Silas.

Abruptly, Verity opened her eyes properly, her body tensing as her hand rested on the cold empty space on the other half of the bed. Of course. She had known Silas wouldn't be there in bed beside her—he had Honor to think of, after all—but the pristine smoothness of the unused pillow next to her own suggested that he had left her on her own as speedily as he could, not even pausing for a few moments to savour their closeness, and that hurt!

Her happiness and joy evaporated immediately.

Once before, he had left her like this and she had woken up alone. Then, he had returned carrying arms full of flowers and fresh bagels he had bought from a bakery in her New York neighbourhood.

Then they had shared a breakfast of kisses and bagels in her bed.

Then…

But this was now and instinct told her that the reason for his absence from her bed had nothing to do with any plans he had to surprise her with early morning flowers or other gifts of love.

She could hear footsteps on the stairs leading to her bedroom but she knew, even before the door was pushed open and Honor's dark head appeared around it, that they did not belong to Silas.

'Are you awake?' Honor asked her.

Forcing a smile, Verity nodded.

'I wanted you to sleep with *me* last night,' Honor told her reproachfully as she ran across the room and scrambled up onto the bed next to Verity, snuggling up to her.

Automatically Verity reached out her arm to draw her close and hold her. Her body, which such a short space of time ago had felt so good, so female, so loved, now felt cold and empty, her muscles aching and tense. But it wasn't *Honor's* fault that she wasn't her father.

Verity could hear fresh footsteps on the stairs but, unlike Honor's, these stopped halfway and she heard Silas call out, 'Honor… Breakfast…'

'Coming, Dad,' Honor called back, scrambling off the bed and starting to head for the door, and then unexpectedly turning round and rushing back to fling her arms around Verity's neck and give her a brief little girl kiss.

Blinking fiercely, Verity watched her leave. The fact that Silas had not chosen to come into her room had told her everything she needed to know about how he felt about last night, as though she *needed* any extra underlining of the fact that it had meant so little to him.

Fresh tears welled and once again she forced them back, but these had nothing to do with the tenderness she had felt at Honor's kiss.

She might only have the haziest memory of how she and Silas had come to be making love last night—she could remember waking up to the touch of his fingers on her face, the warmth of his body next to hers. Presumably he must have had some reason to come up to her room.

She might not know what that was, but she certainly knew why he had made love to her—made love! Had *sex*, she told herself brutally. She might not be able to remember what had brought him to her bed, but she could certainly remember what had kept him there. She couldn't have made her feelings, her need of him, more plain if she'd written them on a ten-foot banner, she told herself bitterly. He'd have to be made of granite not to have taken what she had so stupidly put on offer for him.

Sexual desire, sexual frustration, could do all manner of things to a man—even make him feel the need for a woman he did not like, never mind love, and that was quite plainly what had happened last night. Silas had used her to vent his sexual frustration. No *wonder* he hadn't stayed with her. No *wonder* he was keeping his distance from her this morning.

The plain, ugly truth was that he had used her and she had let him—and not merely let him but positively encouraged him. And to think that when she'd woken up she had thought…felt…believed…

Would she *never* learn? She had believed once before that he had loved her, cared for her, *about* her, and she had been wrong. Now, here she was, eleven years down the line, still hoping, still feeling…still *loving*.

Verity closed her eyes. No. She did *not* still love him. She could not still love him. She *would* not still love him. She opened them again and stared dully at the wall. Just who did she think she was kidding? She loved him all right!

Drearily she got out of bed and headed for the bathroom. Coming back to town had been a total mistake. And she was not even convinced any more about her real motives in having done so.

Or perhaps she was. *Had* it been at the back of her mind all the time that she would see Silas? Even though she knew he was married to someone else?

She gave a small, hollow groan. She had come back because this was her home, the place where she had grown up.

Once she had dressed, reluctantly she made her way downstairs.

When she pushed open the kitchen door, Honor was seated at the table eating her cereal whilst Silas stood at the counter making coffee.

As she walked in he turned and looked at her and then looked quickly away again.

'I've just checked with the garage. They're going to make picking up your car a priority,' he told her, his attention on the kettle he was refilling, asking her briefly, 'Tea or coffee?'

'Coffee, please,' Verity responded. Did he really need to ask? Had he really forgotten how he had teased her in the past about her urgent need for her morning caffeine, or was he underlining the fact that, although her preferences mattered, they were of as little importance to him as she was herself.

'I'll drop you off at your place when I take Honor to school,' he told her as he made her coffee.

'Toast…cereal?'

'No, nothing, thanks,' Verity told him coolly.

As he brought the coffee to her she deliberately turned away from him. He smelled of soap and coffee and her stomach muscles churned frantically as he stood next to her. Inside she was trembling and she had to wrap both her hands around the mug of coffee he had brought her, just in case he might see how much he was affecting her.

*   *   *

'When are we going to do the shopping for the dinner party?' Honor was keen to know.

They were in Silas' car on the way to Honor's school, Verity seated in the front passenger seat next to Silas, at Honor's insistence and very much against her own inclinations. The dinner party! Verity had forgotten all about that.

'That's enough, Honor,' Silas told her crisply as he pulled up at the school gate.

As she hopped out of the car Honor said, 'Look, there's my friend Catherine. I want her to meet you,' and then she was tugging open Verity's door and leaving Verity with no alternative other than to unfasten her seat belt and go with her to where the young girl was standing watching.

'Catherine, this is Verity,' Honor announced importantly. Catherine was smaller and fairer than Honor and it was plain to see which of them was the leader of their twosome, Verity acknowledged as Catherine gave her a shy look and started to giggle.

'Goodbye.' Honor reached up and gave Verity a fierce hug before telling her, 'And don't forget, will you, about the dinner party?'

Verity watched her race out of sight with her friend before turning to walk back to the car. Bending down, she told Silas through the open window, 'I can walk home from here, thank you…'

And before he could say anything she turned smartly on her heel and proceeded to do just that.

She wasn't going to give him another opportunity to humiliate her by keeping his distance from her, she decided proudly, as she lifted her chin and willed herself not to look back at him.

As he watched Verity walking away through his rear-view mirror, Silas hit the steering wheel with the flat of his hand.

He was the one who was in danger of being hurt, rejected, used, so how come it was *Verity* who was behaving as though he were the one treating her badly?

He had known all along that last night had been a mistake and there, this morning, was the proof of it. Verity was treating him as distantly as though they were two strangers. It was perfectly obvious that she regretted what had happened between them, and that she intended to make it very plain to him that neither it nor he meant anything to her. Last night she might have wanted him, but this morning...

'But you promised...' Honor insisted, tears clustering on her lashes as she stared across the table at her father.

'Honor. I've just explained. I don't have the time to get involved in giving dinner parties and—'

'*Verity's* going to do it...'

'*Verity* is far too busy with her own life to want to get involved in ours,' Silas told her curtly. 'And, whilst we're on the subject, I want you to promise me that you won't go round there any more. Verity has her own life to live.'

Watching the tears run pathetically down his daughter's face, Silas cursed silently to himself.

He hated having to disappoint and hurt her like this but what other option did he have? The more he allowed her to get involved with Verity, the more she was going to be hurt in the end.

'Now hurry up and finish your homework,' Silas admonished her sternly. 'I've got to go out at eight and Mrs Simmonds is coming round to babysit you…'

'Mrs Simmonds.' Honor glared at him. She liked the elderly widow who normally came to sit with her on the rare occasions when Silas went out in the evening, but she wasn't Verity.

'Why can't I have Verity? Where are you going anyway?' she demanded suspiciously. 'Not to see Myra?'

Silas gritted his teeth.

'No. I am not.'

He knew perfectly well what was in Honor's mind. She had made it more than plain that she didn't want Myra as a stepmother—not that there had been any real danger of that happening. Myra was not good stepmother material, Silas acknowledged, especially not for Honor who needed a much more compassionate hand on the reins; a much more gentle touch—like Verity's! Now where had that thought come from?

Watching him under her lashes, Honor held her breath. For her, Verity would make the perfect stepmother. She remembered the message she had seen on the back of the photo in her father's desk.

'To my beloved Silas, with all my love for ever and always.'

'Why did they say they didn't know each other, do you suppose?' Catherine had asked, wide-eyed, when Honor had related this interesting fact to her.

Honor had rolled her eyes and told her severely, 'Because they're still in love with one another stupid…'

'How can they be?' Catherine had objected naively. 'Your father married your mother…'

'It happens!' Honor had assured her wisely.

'Maybe they just stopped being in love,' Catherine had suggested, adding, 'Anyway, why do you want to have Verity as your step-mother?'

'Because...' Honor had told her with quelling dismissal.

If she had to have a stepmother, and it seemed that she did, then Verity was quite definitely the one she wanted, and so she had mounted her own special campaign towards that end.

Now, though, things weren't going at all according to plan and the tears filling her eyes weren't entirely manufactured. Cuddled up in Verity's arms this morning, she had experienced an emotion which had broken through the tough, protective outer shell she had created around herself. From being very young she had resented the pity she had seen in the eyes of the women who had cooed at her father and said how hard it must be for him to bring up a little girl like her on his own, scowling horribly at them when she had digested what they'd been saying. Gradually, she had come to see the adult members of her own sex not as potential allies, but as adversaries who wanted to come between her and her father.

With Verity it was different. Honor didn't know why. She just knew that it was, that there was something soft and comforting and lovely about Verity and about being with her. She now wanted Verity as her stepmother, not just to protect her from the likes of Myra, but for herself as herself, and now, just as things were beginning to work out, here was her father being awkward and upsetting all her plans.

His suggestion that Verity might be too busy with her own life to have time for her was one she dismissed out of hand. She knew, of course, that it wasn't true. Verity *liked* her. She could see it in her eyes when she looked at her; there was no mistaking that special loving look. She had seen it in Catherine's mother's eyes when *she* looked at Catherine and felt envious of her because of it.

Silas was driving past Verity's house on his way home. Her BMW was parked in the drive.

On impulse he stopped his own car and got out.

The gardens looked very much the same now as they had done when he had worked in them. There was the border he had been working on the first time he had seen Verity. Grimly he looked away and then, almost against his will, he found himself turning back, walking across the lawn.

The house might have changed since she had lived here, but the gardens hadn't, Verity acknowledged as she paused by the fish pond, peering into it in the dusk of the summer's evening.

Her uncle had used to threaten to have it filled in, complaining that the carp attracted the attentions of a local tom-cat, but Verity had pleaded with him not to do so. She used to love sitting here watching the fish. It was one of her favourite places.

From here she could see the small summer house where she and Silas had exchanged their first earth-shattering kiss.

An unexpected miaow made her jump and then put her hand on her heart as, out of the shadows of the shrubbery, a small, black cat stalked, weaving his way towards her to rub purringly against her legs.

Laughing, Verity bent to stroke him.

'Well, *you* certainly aren't old Tom,' she told him as she rubbed behind his ear, 'but you could be one of his offspring.'

Miaowing as if in assent, the cat jumped up onto the stone edge of the pond where she was sitting and peered into the darkness of the water.

'Ah ha. Yes, you definitely *must* be related to him,' Verity teased.

As a child she would have loved a pet but her uncle had always refused, and once she had become adult the business had kept her too busy and away from home too often for her to feel it would be fair for her to have one.

Now, though, things were different. When she finally decided where she was going to spend the rest of her life, there was nothing to stop her having a cat or a dog if she so chose...

A cat, I suppose it would have to be, she mused. After all, cats and lonely single women were supposed to go together weren't they? A dog somehow or other suggested someone with friends, a family...a full, vigorous life.

Bending her head over the cat, she tickled behind his ear.

'Verity...'

'Silas...' Quickly Verity stood up, her stance unknowingly defensive as though she was trying to hold him off, Silas noted, as she held her hands up in front of her body.

Immediately he took a step back from her.

He couldn't even bear to be within feet of her, never mind inches, Verity recognised achingly as she saw the way Silas distanced himself from her.

'I was just thinking that this cat could be one of old Tom's descendants,' she told Silas huskily, trying to fill the tensioned silence.

'Mmm...from the looks of him he very probably is,' Silas agreed.

'Look, Verity, I wonder if I could have a few words with you.'

Verity's heart sank.

'Yes... Yes, of course,' she managed to agree. Whatever it was Silas wanted to say to her, she could see from his expression that it wasn't anything particularly pleasant.

'It's about Honor,' Silas told her, still keeping his distance from her. 'I've had a talk with her this evening about...about the way she's...she's been trying to involve you in our lives... I've explained to her that *you* have your own life to live and—'

'You've come here to tell me that you don't want her to see me any more,' Verity interrupted flatly, guessing what he was about to say and praying that he wouldn't be able to tell just how much what he was saying was hurting her.

'I... I think it would be best if she didn't,' Silas agreed heavily. 'She's at a very vulnerable age and...'

'Do you think that *I* don't know that?' Verity told him swiftly, her face paling with the intensity of her emotions. 'I've been there, Silas,' she advised him jerkily, 'remember...?'

It was the wrong thing to say, the very worst thing she could have said, she realised as she saw his mouth twist and heard the inflection in his voice as he told her curtly, 'Yes, *I* remember... Honor's got it into her head that she needs a woman's influence in her life,' Silas admitted slowly, 'but...'

'But there's no way you want that woman to be *me*,' Verity guessed angrily.

'I don't want Honor to be *hurt*,' Silas interrupted her bluntly.

Verity stared at him. She could feel the too-fast beat of her own heart and wondered dizzily if Silas too could hear the sound it made as it thudded against her chest wall.

Was he really trying to imply that *she* would stoop so low as to try to hurt *Honor*? A *child*...? Did he really think...?

For a moment Verity felt too outraged to speak. Quickly she swallowed, drawing herself up to her full height as she challenged him, 'Are you suggesting that *I* would hurt Honor? Is that *really* what you think of me, Silas?' she questioned him carefully. 'Do you really think of me as being so...so *vengeful*?'

Half blinded by the tears that suddenly filled her eyes, she turned away from him and started to walk quickly towards the house, breaking into a run when she heard him calling her name.

'Verity,' Silas protested, cursing himself under his breath. She had every right to be angry with him, he knew that. But surely she could see that he had every right to protect his child?

'Verity,' he protested again, but he knew it was too late. She was already running up the steps and into the house.

Quickly Verity dabbed at her hot face with the cold water she had run to stop her tears.

How *could* Silas imply that she would hurt Honor? How *dared* he imply it after what *he* had done to her, the way *he* had hurt *her*? It must be his own guilty conscience that was motivating him.

She would *never* do anything like that. Not to a child, not to *anyone*... She had wanted to help Honor for Honor's sake alone. Her sense of kinship with her had nothing to do with the fact that she was his daughter.

Hadn't it? Slowly she straightened up and looked at herself in the bathroom mirror. Hadn't a part of her recognised how easily *she* might have been Honor's mother? Hadn't she felt somehow honour-bound herself to reach out and help the girl because of that inner knowledge?

To *help* her, yes, but to *hurt* her, never. Never...never...

She couldn't stay here in this town. Not after this. She would ring the agent tomorrow, tell him that she was terminating her lease on the house; the charitable trust she had wanted to establish in her uncle's name in the town could still go ahead—the details of that could be dealt with as easily from London as from here. She had been a fool ever to have come back. She *was* a fool. A stupid, idiotic, heartbroken fool!

CHAPTER TEN

'VERITY... Verity... It is you, isn't it?'

Verity put down the shopping she had just been about to put in the back of the car and looked uncertainly at the woman hailing her, her face breaking into a warm smile as she recognised a girl who had been at school with her.

'Gwen!' she exclaimed warmly. 'Good heavens. How *are* you...?'

'Fine. If you don't count the fact that I'm thirty-three, ten pounds overweight and just about to do a supermarket shop for a husband and three kids,' the other woman groaned. 'When did you get back to town? You look wonderful, by the way...'

'Only very recently. I—'

'Look, I'm in a bit of a rush now. We've got the in-laws coming round for supper.' She pulled a wry face. 'I'd love to have a proper

251

chat with you, catch up on what you've been doing… Can I give you a ring?'

'Yes. Yes, that would be nice,' Verity acknowledged, quickly writing down her telephone number for her before climbing into her car.

It was ironic that she should bump into one of the few girls she had made friends with at school just as she had decided she was going to leave town, she thought as she started her car.

Honor looked sideways at the telephone in the garden centre office. It was Saturday morning and, instead of going swimming with Catherine and her mother, she had opted to come to work with her father. He was outside dealing with a customer. Glancing over her shoulder, Honor reached for the telephone receiver and quickly punched in Verity's telephone number.

Verity heard the telephone ringing as she unlocked the front door, putting down her bag as she went to answer it.

'Verity, is that you?'

Her heart lurched as she recognised Honor's voice and heard its forlorn note.

'Honor… Where are you? Are you all right?' she asked anxiously.

'Mmm…sort of… I'm at the garden centre. Verity, can I come and see you?'

Verity leaned back against the hall wall and closed her eyes.

'Oh, Honor,' she whispered sadly beneath her breath. Opening her eyes, she said as steadily as she could, 'Honor, I don't think that would be a good idea, do you? I—'

'You've spoken to Dad, haven't you?' Honor demanded in a flat, accusing voice. 'I thought you *liked* me… I thought we were *friends*…'

Verity could hear the tears in her voice.

'Honor,' she pleaded. 'Please…'

'I thought you *liked* me…' Honor was repeating, crying in earnest now.

Verity pushed her hand into her hair. She had left it down this morning, oblivious to the admiring male glances she had attracted as she'd walked across the supermarket car park, the bright sunlight burnishing it to honey-gold.

'Honor. Honor, I do... I do...but I shan't be staying in town very much longer. I only intended to make a very short visit here,' Verity began, but Honor was no longer listening to her.

'You're leaving? No, you can't. You mustn't. I need you, Verity.' Then the phone went down.

Leaning against the wall, Verity took a deep breath.

Honor looked at her father. He was still talking to his customer. Sometimes grown-ups just didn't know what was good for them!

She went up to him.

'Dad, I've changed my mind and I want to go swimming with Catherine after all.'

'All right,' Silas agreed. 'Give me five minutes and then I'll drive you round to Catherine's.'

'I'll need to go home first to get my swimming things,' Honor reminded him.

'Fine...' Silas replied.

He was well aware that he was in his daughter's bad books—and why. His only comfort was that one day she would understand and thank him for protecting her. One day...but quite definitely not *today*.

'So what are you going to do?' Catherine asked Honor interestedly. They were sitting in Catherine's bedroom eating Marmite sandwiches and drying one another's hair after their trip to the leisure centre.

'I don't know yet,' Honor replied in despair.

'You could always try to find someone else to be your stepmother,' Catherine suggested cautiously.

'I don't *want* anyone else,' Honor retorted passionately. 'Would you want to change your mother?'

Catherine looked at her.

'Sometimes I would,' she reflected. 'Specially when she won't let me stay up late to watch television.'

*   *   *

'Goodbye, Honor.'

Honor turned dutifully to smile and wave as she got out of Catherine's mother's car.

The latter had just brought her home and Honor could see her father opening the front door for her. Dragging her bag behind her, she headed towards him.

'No kiss for me…?' Silas asked her with forced joviality as she stalked past him and into the house.

Honor turned to give him a withering, womanly look.

'Honor, I was thinking, you know that puppy you wanted…'

'I don't want a puppy,' Honor told him coldly. 'I want *Verity*.'

Silas gritted his teeth. He knew when he was being punished and given the cold-shoulder treatment. How best to handle it? In situations like this he'd benefit from a woman's advice. Verity's? He checked abruptly. Damn Honor. Now she'd got him doing it.

'I've got your favourite for supper,' he told her heartily as he followed her into the kitchen.

'I'm not hungry,' Honor replied. 'We're having an end-of-term play at school... I'm going to be a pop singer but I'm going to have to have a costume.'

'Well, I'm sure we'll be able to find you one,' Silas offered, ignoring for the moment the dubious merits of a ten-year-old aping the manners of a much older pop-singer star, sensing that he was being led onto very treacherous ground indeed, but not as yet quite sure just where the danger was coming from. He soon found out.

'All the other girls are having outfits made by their mothers,' Honor informed him.

'Well, perhaps Mrs Simmonds might...' Silas began, but it was obvious that Honor was not going to be so easily put off.

'*Verity* would know how to make mine,' she informed him coldly. Silas held his breath.

'Now, look, Honor—' he began, but as he watched his daughter's eyes fill with tears which then ran slowly down her face he closed his eyes. This was the very situation which he had hoped to avoid.

'Honor,' he began more gently, but his daughter was refusing to listen to him, whirling round and running out of the room and upstairs.

Silas heard the slam of her bedroom door and sighed.

Verity...

God, but even thinking her name hurt, and not just on Honor's account.

Ever since the night she had spent here he had been fighting not to think about her, not to give in to his compelling, compulsive urge to relive every single second of the time he had held her in his arms, every single heartbeat...

Closing his eyes, he acknowledged what he had been fighting to deny ever since he had walked away, leaving her alone in bed.

It was too late to tell himself not to fall into the trap of loving her again. It had always been too late, for the simple reason that he had never stopped.

'Honor, I've got to go out for half an hour. Will you be all right or shall I phone Mrs Simmonds?'

Honor looked up from the book she was reading. It was Monday teatime and Silas had just received a phone call from one of his customers who wanted to see him urgently.

'No, I'll be fine,' Honor assured him instantly.

Honor waited until she was sure her father had gone before going into the study and rifling through his desk until she found what she was looking for. Yes, there it was, the photograph of Verity.

Picking it up, she turned it over, quickly reading the message on the back.

Desperate situations called for desperate measures. Squaring her shoulders, she went upstairs to her bedroom and packed a haversack with a change of clothes. In the kitchen she added a bar of chocolate to it and then, after thoughtful consideration, added another—for Verity.

Having packed her bag, she then sat down and wrote her father a brief note.

Slowly she read it.

'I am going to live with Verity.'

*   *   *

It didn't take her very long to walk round to Verity's, but even her stout heart gave a small bound of relief when she finally got there and saw that Verity's car was outside. She wasn't sure what she would have done if Verity hadn't been in.

The unexpected ring on the doorbell brought Verity to the door with a small frown.

'Honor!' she exclaimed as she saw the small lone figure. 'What…?'

'I've come to live with you,' Honor told her stoically, walking quickly into the hall and then bursting into tears and flinging herself into Verity's arms as she told her between sobs, 'It's horrid not being able to see you.'

By the time Verity had managed to calm her down she was comfortably ensconced in the kitchen eating home-made biscuits and drinking juice whilst the cat, who had decided to adopt Verity, sat purring on her knee.

'Honor, you *know* you can't stay here, don't you?' Verity asked her gently. 'Your father—'

'He doesn't care,' Honor interrupted her.

'You know that isn't true,' Verity chided her. 'He loves you very much...'

'Like you love him?' Honor asked her, looking her straight in the eye.

Verity opened her mouth and then closed it again. Her legs, she discovered, had gone strangely weak. She sat down and was soon extremely glad that she had done so.

Honor was rifling through the haversack she had brought in with her. Triumphantly she produced the photograph she had taken from her father's desk.

'I found this,' she told Verity, watching her.

'Oh, Honor,' was all Verity could say as she stared at the familiar picture. She could remember the day Silas had taken it—it was the day after they had made love for the first time and Silas had told her he would always keep the photograph in memory of all that they had shared.

'Not that I shall ever need any reminding,' he had whispered passionately to her as he had abandoned the camera and taken her in his arms.

'It says "To my beloved Silas, with all my love for ever and always",' Honor told her solemnly.

Verity looked away from her.

'Yes. Yes, I know,' she agreed weakly.

'You said you didn't *know* my father…' Honor reminded her.

'Yes. Yes, I know,' Verity agreed again.

'And *he* said that *he* didn't know you, but you wrote here that you love him. Why did you stop loving him, Verity?'

'I… It wasn't…' Verity shook her head. 'It was all a long time ago, Honor.'

'But I want to know,' Honor persisted stubbornly.

Verity shook her head, but she sensed that Honor wasn't going to be satisfied until she had dragged the whole sorry story out of her.

'There isn't a lot *to* know,' she told her. 'Your father and I were young. I thought… He said… I had to go away to New York to work and whilst I was there your father met someone else—your mother…'

*   *   *

Silas cursed as he found the note Honor had left for him. Angrily he picked up his discarded car keys and headed for the door. She was coming home with him right now and no nonsense, and once he got her home he was going to have a serious talk with her—a *very* serious talk.

Parking his car behind Verity's, Silas got out and headed for the front door and then, changing his mind, turned to go around the back of the house instead.

The kitchen door was half open—Verity had been outside hanging out some washing when Honor had arrived. Neither of the two occupants of the room could see him and Silas paused in the act of pushing open the door as he heard Verity saying huskily, 'I thought your father loved me. I didn't know about your mother... I suppose I should have guessed that something was wrong when he didn't get in touch with me, but I just thought that he...that he was cross with me because...' She stopped and shook her head. 'I came home to tell him how much I loved him, to tell him that he was

right and that our love was more important
than any duty I owed my uncle, but I discovered that your father had married your mother.'

Helplessly Verity spread her hands.

'I thought he loved me but he didn't really
love me at all.' Her voice shook with emotion
and the cat stopped purring.

Honor looked up, her eyes widening as she
saw her father standing in the doorway.

Verity turned round to see what had attracted Honor's attention, her face paling as
she too saw Silas.

For a moment none of them spoke and then
Silas marched across the room and took hold
of Honor's arm, saying firmly to her, 'Honor,
you're coming with me—right now and no arguments.'

He hadn't said a word to Verity. He hadn't
even looked at her, Verity acknowledged as he
walked Honor out of the back door, firmly
closing it behind him.

She could hear the engine of his car firing.
Her hand shook as she reached across the table
for the photograph that Honor had left.

Tears blurred her eyes. Tipping back her head, she blinked them away. She was not going to cry...not now, not again...not ever...

Catherine's mother looked surprised when she opened the door to find Silas and Honor outside.

'Jane, I'm sorry to do this to you but something very urgent's cropped up. Can Honor stay with you for...until I can get back for her...?'

'Of course she can,' she agreed warmly, ushering Honor inside. What, she wondered, was going on? There had been a lot of whispering being done between the two girls recently and Catherine was rather obviously 'big with news', as the saying went, announcing importantly to anyone who would listen that she and Honor had a special secret.

Having coldly inclined her cheek for her father to kiss, Honor marched inside with all the regal bearing of a grand dowager—a highly offended grand dowager, Jane Alders reflected ruefully.

Silas, however, was looking far too grim-faced for her to think of questioning him.

Verity was just finishing pegging out the last of the washing she had abandoned when Honor had arrived when Silas came back, walking soft-footed across the grass so that she had no inkling of his presence until she suddenly saw his shadow.

'Si…Silas…' To her chagrin the unexpected shock of seeing him made her stammer. 'Wha…what do you want? What are you doing here?'

'Do you want the abridged version?' Silas asked her tersely and then, shaking his head without waiting for her to respond, he demanded abruptly, '*Why* did you tell Honor that you came from New York to tell me how much you loved me?'

'Because it was the truth,' Verity admitted huskily. Why on earth was he asking her that? What could it possibly matter now?

'No, it isn't,' Silas argued flatly. 'Your *uncle* told me the *truth*. He told me that you had asked him to tell me that you didn't want to see me again; that it was all over between us.'

Verity stared at him. Suddenly she felt extremely cold.

'No,' she whispered, her hand going to her throat. 'No, that's not true, he *couldn't* have told you that. I don't believe it...'

'Believe it,' Silas told her harshly, 'because I can assure you that he did. Not that I was in any mood to listen to him. Not then. I even wrote to you begging you to change your mind, pleading with you to write back to me, giving what I suppose was an ultimatum in that I wrote that if *I* didn't hear from you then I would have to accept that it was over between us.'

Verity badly needed to sit down.

'Is this some kind of joke?' she asked Silas weakly.

His mouth hardened.

'Can you see me laughing?' he demanded.

Verity shook her head. She could see that he was telling her the truth, but the full enormity of just what her uncle had done, of what he had set in motion, was still too much for her to fully comprehend.

'I never got your letter,' she whispered. 'There was a murder in the apartment block and my uncle insisted that I had to move out. He promised me that he would give you my new address and telephone number. I... I waited and waited for you to get in touch and then, when you didn't...for a while I... You were right. Our love was more important than doing what my uncle wanted. I... I came home to tell you that. To tell you how much I loved you and...' To her horror Verity felt hot tears spill down her cheeks as she relived the full trauma of that time.

'I read about your marriage in the taxi on the way from the station. After that I knew there was no point in trying to see you,' she told him bleakly.

Verity looked down at the ground. *Why* was he doing this to her, dragging her through this...this humiliation? What could it matter now?

'Look, let's put aside the issue of my marriage for the moment,' she heard Silas telling her huskily. 'I want to concentrate on something else, on something far more important... Did you really love me so much, Verity?'

For a moment she was tempted to lie, but why should she? Proudly she lifted her head and looked at him.

'Yes. I did,' she acknowledged. 'I...' Quickly she swallowed, knowing that she could not admit to him that she had never stopped loving him; that she still loved him and that, if anything, that love was even deeper and more painful to her now than it had been then.

'I didn't marry Sarah because I loved her,' she heard Silas telling her rawly. 'I married her because she was pregnant.'

Disbelievingly, Verity focused on him.

'But...' she whispered, shaking her head. 'You would never do something like that. You would never make love to someone you didn't...you didn't care about...'

'I didn't make love to her,' he told her bluntly. 'We just had sex.'

Briefly, without allowing her to stop him, Silas told her exactly what had happened.

After he had finished speaking Verity looked searchingly into his eyes. There was no doubting the veracity of what he had just told her. Her stomach felt as though it had just done a fast cycle in a washing machine, her heart was banging so hard against her ribs she thought it was going to break them, and as for her legs…

'I…I need to sit down,' she told Silas weakly.

'And I need to lie down,' he countered gruffly, 'preferably in bed with you in my arms with nothing between us, with nothing to separate us. Oh, Verity,' he groaned as he suddenly reached for her, wrapping her in his arms as he kissed her eyes, her face, her mouth. 'Oh, Verity, Verity,' he whispered rawly to her. 'You are the only woman I've ever loved, the only woman I ever *will* love…'

'No, that can't be true,' Verity whispered back through kiss-swollen lips. 'It can't be... Not after the way you left me the other night...not after I'd begged you to stay...'

Tears filled her eyes and rolled down her cheeks.

'Oh, no, my darling, don't cry. Please don't cry.' Silas groaned, holding her tight and rocking her in his arms, his cheek pressed against her head. 'It wasn't like that, it really wasn't. I left you because...because I was afraid, not just for myself or for the pain I knew I would feel if I let you back into my life, but for the pain I thought you might cause Honor.'

'I would *never* hurt Honor,' Verity protested fiercely.

'No,' Silas agreed softly. 'Forgive me for that.'

'She reminds me so much of the way I was...' Verity told him shakily. 'Oh, I know how much you love her, Silas...and you *couldn't* be more different from my uncle—'

'But I'm not enough,' Silas interrupted her ruefully, adding before she could protest, 'I know, so my darling daughter has already informed me.'

'Did you really think that of me…that I might hurt you both…?'

'You'd already hurt me very badly once,' Silas reminded her softly. 'Or, at least, so I thought.'

'I felt the same way about you,' Verity admitted. 'It hurt so much knowing that when you'd told me you loved me, when you said that you'd love me for ever, you didn't mean it…'

'I *did* mean it,' Silas corrected her. 'I still mean it, Verity. Is it too late for us to start again?' he asked her seriously.

Verity looked at him, her heart in her eyes.

'I… Oh, Silas…' she whispered.

'Let's go inside,' he whispered back. 'There's a phone call I want to make…'

Even to make his telephone call to Jane Alders, Silas refused to let Verity move out of his arms.

'You stay right where you are,' he mock growled at her when she did try to move away.

'Jane, it's Silas,' he announced when Catherine's mother answered his call, tucking the receiver in the crook of his neck whilst he bent his head to feather a soft kiss against Verity's mouth. 'Would it be asking too much for you to keep Honor there with you tonight? I wouldn't ask but... You don't mind...? No, it's okay, I don't need to speak with her,' he continued, 'but if you could just give her a message from me, if you wouldn't mind. Could you tell her that I think she might be going to get what she wanted? What she wanted more than a puppy,' he stressed, smiling.

'What was all that about?' Verity asked him when he had replaced the receiver.

Smiling at her, Silas said, 'Honor has been begging and pleading with me to let her have a puppy. The other day when I ill-advisedly offered her one as a peace-offering, she informed me that she didn't want a puppy, she wanted you.'

Verity looked at him.

'Oh, Silas,' she protested, torn between laughter and tears.

'I want to take you to bed,' Silas told her huskily, cupping her face in both his hands. 'I want to make love to you, Verity... I want to make love with you. I want to re-affirm all those vows and promises we made to each other years ago, but if you think it is too soon, if you want to wait...if you feel...'

Putting her fingertips against his lips to silence him, Verity told him softly, 'What I feel right now is that I want you. I want you in all the ways that a woman wants a man she loves, Silas. You can't imagine how empty my life has been without you, how—'

'Can't I?' he checked her gruffly. 'There hasn't been a day in the years we've been apart when *I* haven't thought about you. Even on the day of Sarah's funeral... As I stood at her graveside all I could think was how much I needed and wanted you.'

'Poor girl,' Verity whispered compassionately.

'Yes, poor girl,' Silas agreed.

'Take me to bed,' Verity begged him urgently. 'Take me to bed, Silas, and...'

She didn't have to say any more, *couldn't* have said any more because suddenly he was picking her up and carrying her towards the stairs.

'You are the most beautiful woman on earth,' Silas whispered extravagantly as he threaded his fingers through Verity's hair.

Smiling lazily up at him in the aftermath of their lovemaking, Verity reached out and touched his face, wriggling appreciatively against the muscled warmth of his naked body.

'Hey, don't do that,' Silas warned her as he slowly kissed the palm of her hand. 'At least, not unless you want...'

'Not unless I want what?' Verity teased, deliberately moving even closer.

'Not unless you want this,' Silas told her huskily, taking her hand and placing it against his hardening body.

'Silas, we can't,' Verity protested unconvincingly as her fingers stroked instinctively down the hard strength of the silky, hot-skinned shaft of male pleasure she was caressing.

It felt so good to be able to touch him like this, to know how much he wanted and needed her, to know how much he loved her.

'Oh, no?' Silas challenged softly, cupping her breast in his hand and bending his head to trail tiny provocative kisses all the way down from her collar-bone to her navel.

'Don't...' Verity whispered.

'Don't what?' Silas asked her as he circled her navel with the tip of his tongue, gently biting at her flesh.

'Don't...don't stop,' Verity breathed.

'I'm not going to,' Silas assured her as his head dipped lower and his hand slid between her thighs.

This was bliss, heaven, every delight she had ever known or imagined knowing, Verity decided shakily as she gave in to the gentle caress of Silas' hand against her body and the slow, sensual search of his mouth as it homed in on the sensitive female heart of her.

The orgasmic contractions gripping her body were, if anything, even stronger this second time. Just for a second she tried to resist them, wanting to share what she was experiencing with Silas, but he wouldn't let her.

'Let it happen, Verity,' he begged her, his voice shaking with male arousal. 'I want to see it happen for you, feel it happen…'

'Silas,' she protested, but it was already too late. With a small cry she gave in to the urgency of Silas' plea and her body's own demands.

'Have you thought…?' Silas questioned her later, when they were sitting up in bed eating the smoked salmon sandwiches he had gone down to make for them and drinking the bottle of white wine they had decided would have to stand in lieu of celebratory champagne.

They probably looked more like a couple of naughty children, sitting side by side in the nest they had made of the duvet and pillows, Verity acknowledged, than adults, but she felt almost childlike, full of all the youthful hope and shining joy that she had lost when she had thought she had lost Silas. She felt, she recognised, like a girl again, only this time she was able to appreciate what she had, what they had, with all the maturity of a woman.

'Have I thought what?' she prompted, taking a bite of the sandwich he was proffering her and giggling when he withdrew it so that her teeth grazed his skin, and then teasingly licking at his fingers as though she hadn't known all along that that was just what he'd wanted her to do.

'Mmm…' he retaliated, bending to nibble on her own fingertips. 'Tastes good, but not as good as—'

'Silas,' Verity reproved. 'Have I thought what?'

'Well, I don't know about you,' he told her seriously, 'but I certainly wasn't using any precautions.' He shook his head. 'To be truthful, that was the last thing on my mind, irresponsible though it sounds.'

Verity gave him a concerned look.

'I'm not protected from conceiving,' she admitted, adding semi-shyly, 'I don't... Well, there's never been any need, not since... Not since, well, not since you and I...'

The sandwiches were pushed to one side as he took her in his arms and groaned.

'Oh, Verity, I never expected... I couldn't, and I love you just the same no matter what... Have you any idea just how much that means to me? It's the same for me, you know,' he told her quietly. 'I haven't...'

'Not even with Myra?' Verity asked him.

'Most especially not with Myra.' Silas grinned.

'She wanted you,' Verity told him.

'Mmm...but she didn't get me. There wasn't anything here for her,' he told her seriously, touching his own heart lightly and then adding, 'and so there couldn't be anything here either...' Verity watched as he touched his sex.

'I thought it didn't work like that for men,' was all she could manage to say.

'For some men, but not for me. Perhaps that's why I'm so hungry for you now,' he told her with a soft groan. 'I've got a lot of lonely nights to make up for…'

'I don't want to get pregnant,' Verity told him, explaining when she saw the look in his eyes, 'I mean, not just yet. Not until Honor has had a chance to…to adjust…to know that she'll always be very special to both of us… We need time together as a unit, a family… We need to bond properly together as a three-some, Silas, before we introduce a new baby into our family. We owe it to Honor to wait until *she's* ready.'

When she looked at him she saw that his eyes were bright with emotion.

'What is it?' she asked him warily. 'Have I…?'

'You're perfect, just perfect, do you know that?' he told her passionately. 'No wonder Honor is so determined to have you as her stepmother. Come here and let me kiss you…'

Smiling at him, Verity complied…

EPILOGUE

'WHAT are you doing?' Catherine asked Honor curiously.

They were both standing in Verity's bedroom, still wearing their bridesmaid's dresses from the afternoon wedding ceremony which had taken place in the garden. Honor was writing something down on a piece of paper, shielding it with her hand as she kept a weather eye on the half-open bedroom door.

Down below them, in the garden, Verity and Silas were mingling with their guests, Silas' arm wrapped protectively around his new wife's waist.

'I'm writing a list of babies' names,' Honor informed her friend loftily.

'Babies names... What for? *You* won't be having a baby for ages yet,' Catherine told her.

'It's not for me, stupid,' Honor told her. 'It's for Verity.'

'Is Verity having a baby?' Catherine asked her, looking confused.

'Maybe not quite yet. But she soon will be now that she and Dad are married,' Honor told her confidently. 'I think, if it's a girl we should call her Mel and if it's a boy...I think Adam...'

'Why Adam?' Catherine asked her.

'It's a nice name for a baby brother.'

Down below them in the garden, happily oblivious to the plans that were being made for their future, Verity leaned a little closer into Silas' body.

'Looking forward to tonight?' he teased her wickedly as he felt the soft warmth of her body.

Laughing ruefully, Verity wrinkled her nose at him.

'You're the one who's supposed not to be able to wait to get *me* into bed, not the other way around,' she reminded him.

'What makes you think I'm not?' Silas challenged her. 'We're going to have to make the most of tonight,' he warned her. 'It's the last night we're going to have to ourselves for quite some time.'

'Mmm... I know,' Verity agreed, closing her eyes as she dwelt blissfully on the thought of the luxurious suite at the hotel where he had once made love to her that Silas had booked in their names for their wedding night. She smiled as she remembered that on their first stay there they had a much smaller room.

'If I ever thought about where I'd spend a honeymoon, it certainly wasn't Disneyland,' he told Verity dryly.

She opened her eyes and laughed.

'No, me neither,' she admitted.

'So how come *you* were the one who insisted that we make the booking?' Silas asked her gently. 'Or can I guess?'

'We couldn't have gone away without her,' she told him quickly.

'Maybe *you* couldn't,' Silas agreed roundly, 'but I certainly could!'

'You don't mean that.'

'Don't I?' He gave her a wide, almost boyish grin that made him look heartachingly young. 'We must be mad. Three *weeks* in Disneyland with Honor in tow…'

'Either that or we must be grateful,' Verity acknowledged, whispering the words into a soft kiss. 'After all, without her…'

'Yes,' he admitted. 'Without her…'

Both of them glanced up towards Verity's open bedroom window where they could hear the sound of raised voices.

'Well, I think Adam is a stupid name for a baby,' Catherine was shouting.

'I don't care what *you* think,' Honor was retaliating in an equally loud voice. 'I like it and he's going to be *my* brother.'

Her what? Verity and Silas looked at one another whilst all around them their guests started to grin.

'Honor,' Silas began sternly.

Verity touched his arm and shook her head.

'Don't say anything to her,' she begged him. 'I think this is probably my fault.'

'Your fault? How can it be?'

'She came into the bathroom this morning whilst I was being sick,' Verity told him quietly.

'You were being *sick*…?' Silas stared at her, his face changing colour and then becoming suffused with tender emotion as he took hold of her gently and asked, 'Are you?'

'I don't know…not yet… But Honor seems to have made up her mind what *she* thinks if it proves to be true,' she told him ruefully. 'She was thrilled—so much for us waiting.'

Silas gave a small sigh.

'You do realise that this baby is going to make her completely impossible, don't you?' He groaned. 'She'll never let either of us near her or him…'

Glancing towards the upper window and her small stepdaughter, Verity smiled.

'She's going to be the best sister that any baby could have,' she told him softly—and meant it.

MILLS & BOON® PUBLISH EIGHT
LARGE PRINT TITLES A MONTH.
THESE ARE THE EIGHT TITLES
FOR SEPTEMBER 1999

❦

THE PATERNITY AFFAIR
Robyn Donald

THE SPANISH GROOM
Lynne Graham

THE UNEXPECTED BABY
Diana Hamilton

WANTING HIS CHILD
Penny Jordan

NELL'S COWBOY
Debbie Macomber

MARRIAGE ON THE EDGE
Sandra Marton

HER GUILTY SECRET
Anne Mather

AN INNOCENT BRIDE
Betty Neels

MILLS & BOON®

Makes any time special™

MILLS & BOON® PUBLISH EIGHT
LARGE PRINT TITLES A MONTH.
THESE ARE THE EIGHT TITLES
FOR OCTOBER 1999

———————— ❧ ————————

HAVING HIS BABIES
Lindsay Armstrong

THE MARRIAGE QUEST
Helen Brooks

THE SECRET MISTRESS
Emma Darcy

LOVER BY DECEPTION
Penny Jordan

ONE HUSBAND REQUIRED!
Sharon Kendrick

LONE STAR BABY
Debbie Macomber

THE TYCOON'S BABY
Leigh Michaels

A NINE-TO-FIVE AFFAIR
Jessica Steele

MILLS & BOON®

Makes any time special™